This time she wasn't giving in.

Christina scanned the page, smiling as she read the names of two past Louisiana Derby winners, Black Gold and Grindstone, who had gone on to win the Kentucky Derby.

"The Louisiana Derby is emerging as an important prep race for the Championship Series races," the description read. "Early nominations include acclaimed horses from across the United States." *And the purse would pay the farm's taxes and then some,* Christina thought. But even more important, if Star won this race, he'd prove he had the stuff to run in the Kentucky Derby. Maybe her mom was right after all: Fair Grounds *was* perfect for Star.

There was just one problem. Her mother wanted to enter Star in a small stakes race. When Ashleigh had mentioned Fair Grounds, the Louisiana Derby wasn't what she'd had in mind.

But this time I'm not giving in, Christina thought, gearing up for another battle of wills.

Collect all the books in the Thoroughbred series

Collect all the books in the Ashleigh series

* coming soon

THOROUGHBRED

RISING STAR

CREATED BY
JOANNA CAMPBELL

WRITTEN BY
KARLE DICKERSON

HarperEntertainment
An Imprint of HarperCollinsPublishers

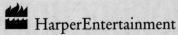

HarperEntertainment
An Imprint of HarperCollins*Publishers*
10 East 53rd Street, New York, NY 10022-5299

This is a work of fiction. The characters, incidents, and dialogues are products of the author's imagination and are not to be construed as real. Any resemblance to actual events or persons, living or dead, is entirely coincidental.

Produced by 17th Street Productions, an Alloy Online, Inc., company

HarperCollins books are available at special quantity discounts for bulk purchases for sales promotions, premiums, or fund-raising. For information please call or write: Special Markets Department, HarperCollins Publishers Inc., 10 East 53rd Street, New York, NY 10022. Telephone: (212) 207-7528. Fax: (212) 207-7222.

ISBN 0-06-106824-1

HarperCollins®, ®, and HarperEntertainment™ are trademarks of HarperCollins Publishers Inc.

Cover art © 2001 by 17th Street Productions, an Alloy Online, Inc., company

First printing: October 2001

Printed in the United States of America

Visit HarperEntertainment on the World Wide Web at
www.harpercollins.com

❖ 10 9 8 7 6 5 4 3 2

To Brandon, Devon, and Morgan

CLAAAAANNNNNNGGGGGGGG!

The bell on the starting gate was stuck, and the din was horrific. Seventeen-year-old Christina Reese put her hands over her ears, trying to keep from being thrown like a rag doll from a madly plunging Wonder's Star, trapped in the chute at Churchill Downs. Couldn't anybody shut it off? What was wrong? Surely the Kentucky Derby wasn't going to be ruined for them by a stuck bell!

Oh, will the noisy thing never shut off?

Christina's eyes flew open, and within a few seconds recognition flooded through her. She was safe in her darkened bedroom at Whitebrook Farm, the Thoroughbred breeding and training operation her parents owned in Lexington, Kentucky. But the loud

1

clamor continued, and it was coming from her cousin Melanie Graham's room. It was Melanie's alarm clock, Christina realized.

Leaping out of bed, Christina gasped as her bare feet hit the cold hardwood floor. Then she headed down the hall to Melanie's bedroom. Melanie was fast asleep, oblivious to the insistent sound emanating from her clock.

Christina shut off the alarm, and her eyes caught sight of the time. "Three-thirty?" she groaned. What was Melanie doing setting her alarm for three-thirty? While it was true that morning came early on a Thoroughbred farm, it certainly didn't start *that* early. It was still nighttime!

"Huh?" Melanie mumbled, sitting up in bed and blinking blearily. Her blond hair was sticking up all over the place. "What was that awful racket? What are you doing in here, Chris?"

Christina glared at her cousin with her hands on her hips. "What are *you* doing setting your alarm to go off in the middle of the night?"

Melanie rubbed her eyes. "I didn't. Oh, yes, I did. I'm supposed to study for math. I was too tired last night. Big test today." She sat up and threw off her covers. "Brrr!" she said, pulling them up to her chin once more. "On second thought, forget the test. Oh, shoot. I can't forget the test. I have a D in math."

Christina sighed heavily. Melanie definitely wasn't a serious student. Always procrastinating, she was barely passing any of her classes. Only the week before, Melanie's dad had called to threaten to ground Melanie from racing if her grades didn't improve.

"Oh, Melanie, how can you possibly study at this hour?" Christina asked, yawning.

"I don't have any choice," her cousin answered grimly. "I was going to study last night. Really, I was. But then Jazz called from Los Angeles, and we were having such a good conversation. Before I knew it, it was too late to hit the books."

Christina smiled. Melanie acted as though she didn't care one bit about Jazz Taylor, the rock star who shared the ownership of Melanie's favorite racehorse, Perfect Image, with Will Graham, Melanie's father. But Christina knew Melanie wouldn't spend one minute on the phone with any guy she didn't have some feelings for.

"I think you'd be better off getting some sleep and faking it," Christina suggested, seeing how tired Melanie looked. "You don't care that much about your grades anyway."

Melanie snorted. "I wish. I totally bombed the last test. I really can't afford to blow this one, too."

She sat up, switched on the lamp on her nightstand, and grabbed her math book. "Sorry I woke you

3

up, Chris. You can go back to bed. Don't worry about me. I'm going to study until you wake up again. I'm determined to ace this test."

Christina didn't need any urging. She padded back to her room and flopped back down on her bed, but it was no use. She was awake for good. There was no way she could go back to sleep. She found herself thinking about the interview she was going to give later that day with a reporter from the *Daily Racing Form*. When her mom had first mentioned the interview featuring her horse, Wonder's Star, Christina had been reluctant. But then she had decided that now was as good a time as any to tell the world about Star's incredible comeback.

It was truly amazing how well Star had done in the past few months, since an undiagnosed illness had nearly taken his life. It had happened at the Belmont track. Another horse stabled nearby had first contracted the disease and shortly thereafter had died of it. Star first showed signs of the illness during a race. He had barely made it across the finish line, well behind the other contenders. He had gone downhill immediately after that and had been returned to Whitebrook. His symptoms had gotten dramatically worse until it looked as though there was no way he was going to pull through.

After weeks of twenty-four-hour care and never-ending worry, Star had made a miraculous recovery from the mysterious ailment. But that hadn't been the end of his and Christina's troubles. Somewhere along the way something had happened to the trust that the two of them had built over the years. Star was misbehaving, and Christina could no longer communicate with him. It had taken a trip to Montana and several hard lessons with Christina's talented friend Lyssa Hynde to reestablish the all-important bond between horse and rider.

Lyssa, who competed against Christina's boyfriend, Parker Townsend, in combined training, had taught Christina the Native American horsemanship techniques that had helped make things right with Star again. With Lyssa's help, Christina had managed to overcome her own stubbornness and learned to talk to Star in a way that he could understand and trust. Christina learned that Star had to trust her leadership or they would never work well together.

"Make him want to follow the *itancan*," Lyssa always said, using a Native American word meaning "leader."

After a few rough episodes, Christina had finally gotten through to Star, and they had been making tremendous progress ever since. Still, her mother, racing legend Ashleigh Griffen, didn't seem to notice that Star had improved so dramatically that he was ready to race in the big leagues again. Ashleigh seemed to think that Star was lucky to be alive and they'd better not push their luck by racing him against any top-caliber horses.

Christina knew that her mom had agreed to the interview only because she knew the racing world was interested in what had happened to Star, who had shown early promise as a Kentucky Derby contender. Christina also realized her mom had given up hope that the chestnut colt would be able to enter the race at all. After all, it was only a few months away.

Just the other day Ashleigh had handed her a local racing schedule. "Look through here. There ought to be a short, less-competitive race for Star in here somewhere," she had suggested.

Less competitive! Christina had tossed the schedule aside without even looking at it. She could see that Ashleigh was pinning her hopes on Melanie's horse, Perfect Image, to be the next Whitebrook horse to run in the Kentucky Derby. She thought Star was still too weak to run against such stiff competition.

Christina knew it was a long shot, but in her heart she hoped that Star would run for the roses. After all, he had been running against the odds ever since his birth, when his dam, Ashleigh's Wonder, had died. He'd overcome every setback in his path since then. Plus in his last few workouts Star had shown that his fire was definitely still there. His times didn't match the best ones he'd run before his illness, but they were steadily improving. Even Ian McLean, Whitebrook's head trainer, had seemed pleased by the last time Star had clocked, just two days before.

"I'll get Mom to see that Star is still Triple Crown material," Christina vowed as she got out of bed and started getting dressed. "He won't run in any wimpy, short races if I can help it!"

It was still only four-thirty, but now that she was awake, she might as well head down to the barn. Pulling on her jeans and a thick, woolen turtleneck, Christina twisted her hair and clipped it up on top of her head. Grabbing her zippered sweatshirt, she made her way down the hall, noticing that Melanie's room was dark. Christina chuckled. Melanie had fallen back to sleep after all. In the kitchen, Christina tucked an apple into her pocket, then slipped silently out the kitchen door and headed toward the barn.

In the eerie yellowish barn light, Christina could see Jonnie, the groom who had night duty, sitting on a bale of straw outside the barn, cupping a steaming mug of coffee in his hands.

"Morning, Chris. You're up before the chickens," he said.

"Yeah," Christina replied, shoving her cold hands into her pockets. "My wake-up call came early today, courtesy of Melanie. She's still sleeping, of course."

Jonnie chuckled as Christina walked past him into the dimly lit barn aisle. "Going to brief Star before his big interview with the folks from the *Racing Form?*" he asked.

Stopping for a moment, Christina wrinkled her brow. "How did you know I had an interview?"

Jonnie sipped his coffee. "How does anyone know anything around here?"

Christina sighed and turned toward Star's stall again. She was always amazed at how quickly news traveled around the farm. Everybody always seemed to know everyone else's business.

Walking softly so as not to disturb the dozing Thoroughbreds, Christina took in the sleepy noises around her. There was a soft rustling in the straw, some stamping of feet, and the occasional rattle of a feed pan, even though it would be some time before the morning feeds began.

When Christina stopped outside Star's stall, she looked in and saw that the big chestnut was not asleep. He was standing eagerly by the door, whickering softly and demanding attention.

"Good morning, big guy," she said, opening the stall door and stepping inside. He nosed her pocket until she withdrew the apple, offering it to him.

She stroked his glossy mane while he crunched the apple calmly. "Guess you couldn't sleep, either," she murmured. "Psyching yourself for the big interview, huh?"

Star grunted softly, as if in reply, and Christina

reached over to scratch him under his jaw. "Well, get ready to dazzle that reporter. It's time we let everyone know that a Derby win is definitely in our plans."

She stood by the big colt for a long while, murmuring softly to him, until she heard another Whitebrook groom, Joe Kisner, starting up the tractor that pulled the harrow around the track. That meant it was time to start getting ready for the morning workouts.

As the stable area came to life, Christina helped Kevin McLean, Ian's son, take several yearlings down to the paddocks. She grimaced as one awkward colt danced sideways into her and managed to step on her foot. She jumped back, twisting her ankle in the process. But her pain was forgotten when she paused for a moment to watch the gangly youngsters gambol around in the roomy enclosures. They staged mock battles with their forefeet, their cloudy breath mingling with the mist rising from the ground. It was cold this early March morning, but the trees were beginning to leaf out, and Christina knew spring was just around the corner.

Spring at Whitebrook meant the tail end of foaling season. But for Christina, it also meant something else—that it was time to make big decisions about her future. At her parents' urging, she had gone through the process of applying to college at the University of Kentucky, where her boyfriend, Parker Townsend, went. But over the last couple of months Christina had come to know with increasing certainty that she wanted nothing more than to race Star. College would have to wait. But how was she ever going to break the news to her mom and dad that she had decided to put off getting a college education so that she could follow her dream of being a world-class jockey?

She had no idea.

"Well, I'm not going to worry about that now. Time to get to work," Christina said aloud.

Heading to the training barn, Christina checked the schedule on the chalkboard to see which horse she would be riding first. She frowned when she saw that none of the horses had been assigned to her.

"No need for the long face."

Christina turned at the sound of the voice behind her. It was Maureen Mack, the assistant trainer. "Catwink and Rascal turned up puffy this morning, so Ian wants to rest them," Maureen explained. "Kevin and Melanie can handle the others. That frees you up for your interview and gives you plenty of time to work Star before school."

"Thanks," Christina replied. She frowned as the ankle she'd just twisted began to throb.

"I'll get Star ready for you," offered Dani, one of Whitebrook's grooms, carrying Christina's light exercise saddle out of the tack room.

"Great," Christina replied. "I'll be right out."

She had just reached for her goggles and helmet when she heard footsteps behind her.

Turning around, she saw her mom walking up with a young woman wearing a crisp gray jacket and pants and carrying a small silver tape recorder.

Ashleigh put her hand on Christina's shoulder. "This is my daughter, Christina Reese. She'll be glad to give you all the information you need. She's raised Star since he was a baby and knows him inside and out."

"Hello," Christina said, reaching over to shake the reporter's hand.

"Brynn Howard," said the reporter briskly.

"Ms. Howard is with the *Racing Reporter*, not the *Daily Racing Form*. I must have misunderstood," Ashleigh said, barely masking her distain.

Christina swallowed a lump of disappointment. The *Daily Racing Form* was the most popular and well-respected racing paper in the business. The *Racing Reporter* had a much smaller circulation. In fact, Christina had never even seen it before. Well, she decided, she might as well start somewhere. Once Star started winning again, the *Daily Racing Form* would be clamoring for an interview, Christina was sure of it.

The reporter strode over quickly and held out her hand. "Christina Reese, the owner of Wonder's Star, son of a Derby and Preakness winner, a horse that till last fall was the talk of the tracks," she said loudly with a voice that fired rapidly like a machine gun. "Your mom filled me in on Wonder's Star's racing record, but I want to know just where he is right now, after his illness, and anything else you can tell me about him."

Ashleigh nodded her head. "Well, I'll be with the broodmares if you need me. Ian's expecting you both at the oval," she said, and headed off.

Christina looked fleetingly after her mom and wished she could duck out of this interview. Her ankle was really beginning to hurt, and she was already irritated with the interviewer's brusque manner. She had a feeling that the interview wasn't going to be quite what she had planned.

Oh, come on. Don't be paranoid, Christina told herself.

She turned to the reporter. "Thanks for coming out so early," she said. "Excuse me—I'll need to take a moment to tape up my ankle before I show you Star."

"Fine by me. I'll just ask you a few questions in the meantime if you don't mind." She looked down as Christina limped for a few steps toward the tack room, where the first-aid kit was kept. "You jockeys are always getting banged up, aren't you?"

Christina tried to ignore the pain in her ankle.

"Some more than others," she replied neutrally while making an effort to walk normally.

The reporter studied her for a moment before adding, "You can tell me all about it. So is it true that behind the scenes Star's a bad actor? I hear he can really give his rider a hard time in his works."

Christina was puzzled. There was no doubt that Star was sensitive and even playful at times. But a bad actor? At every track that she'd taken Star to, people had complimented her on his calm, businesslike behavior. Where had the reporter heard that? "Are you kidding? He's a big teddy bear. Why do you ask?"

Brynn's eyes darted pointedly at Christina's ankle, and she raised a skeptical eyebrow. It took a few seconds, but suddenly Christina realized that the reporter thought Star was involved in her injury. She probably thought Star had deliberately stepped on Christina or something. Sitting on a tack trunk, Christina pulled off a strip of tape and started winding it around her ankle.

"If you mean this, it was purely an accident. A big yearling just stepped on me, that's all. It's no big deal, really," Christina said. She finished taping up her foot, then slipped on her sock and boot again.

The reporter looked disappointed.

She's looking for a juicy story! Christina realized as she started lacing up her paddock boot. Some reporters were like that. They didn't want to hear the real story. They just wanted to come up with a tidbit or two so they could write an article that would get a big headline and grab everyone's attention.

This one probably had a headline or two already written: "Wonder's Star: Putting Away the Competition— or His Rider?" or "Wonder's Star: Backside Brat?"

Luckily, her mom and Cindy McLean, Ian's step-daughter, had coached Christina on how to handle the press. Both of them had raced for years, and both had lots of experience when it came to journalists. "Stick to the facts," Ashleigh always said. "Don't give anything away that you don't have to," Cindy had advised her again and again.

Seeing that Christina wasn't going to say anything more about her ankle, Brynn held up her recorder. "Well, then, I'll fire away." She cleared her throat and began. "So I believe it was *Bloodhorse* magazine that once called him 'Wonder's Wonder Horse'?"

Christina grinned and nodded proudly, remembering.

The reporter rushed on. "It wasn't too long ago that Wonder's Star flagged at Belmont and shortly after was at death's door. Has he completely recovered, and is he really ready to run again?"

"Absolutely yes, to both parts of that question," Christina said firmly. "It's been months since he's been sick, and we've both been working hard. He's almost in top condition, and he's definitely ready to run again."

The reporter's eyes narrowed. "But if it's true they were never able to pinpoint the cause of his illness, how can you be so sure Star won't get sick again?"

"All I know is that there's no reason to think he will," Christina replied in a clipped tone. "He's healthy, and he's been turning in very strong works. His vet is sure that all the danger's over. So now we're moving on. We have big plans for Star."

"Big plans? Do you mind being more specific?"

Christina hesitated. She had been led into blurting out more than she should to the press before and had regretted it. Did she dare spill her plans to enter Star in the Derby? Well, why not? Certainly anyone who knew her knew how important her dream was. And anyone who knew Star had to see that he was up to the challenge. Taking a deep breath, she fixed her gaze on the reporter and stood up.

"We're so confident in Star that we're going ahead with our plans to enter him in the Derby."

"You do mean the *Kentucky* Derby, don't you, Miss Reese?" the reporter asked, thrusting the recorder closer to Christina's face.

Christina felt herself bristling at the reporter's emphasis but forced herself to remain calm. "Yes, of course," she replied evenly.

"From what your mother said, I gathered Star was,

well . . . You do realize the sort of competition you'll be up against, don't you? All the top horses in the country will be there."

Struggling to keep her cool, Christina lifted her chin defiantly. Why had she said anything about the Derby? Her parents wouldn't be happy that she was talking so outrageously about plans she hadn't even discussed with them first.

Oh, why did I ever agree to this interview in the first place? Christina wondered. She should have kept the press away and let them have a glimpse of Star only when he was crossing the finish line at his next race! But in the next moment she remembered why. She had wanted everyone to know just how confident she was that Star was a serious contender.

"I'm well aware of our competitors. It should be a thrilling race," Christina said, trying to sound confident.

"It will certainly be an exciting field. There are people who say this year's crop is stronger than ever. Take Townsend Acres' Celtic Mist, for instance."

"He's definitely one to watch," Christina replied evenly.

"You can say that again. He just keeps winning and winning. Wasn't he something in the Fountain of Youth?"

Christina was silent. Brad Townsend had already

bragged enough about his colt. She was tired of hearing about Celtic Mist.

The reporter went on. "Well, you are surely aware that most people consider your colt a has-been? Just yesterday I was talking to the respected owner of a Derby contender who says he has written Star off completely as a horse to contend with."

Gee, I wonder who that could have been, Christina thought sarcastically, attempting to keep her face from expressing her irate thoughts. *Brad Townsend, perhaps?*

"How does it feel to know that everyone has given up on Star? That maybe the so-called wonder horse just might be a has-been?"

Christina gaped at the reporter, not believing what she had just heard. She felt her temples pounding. At that moment she remembered that Dani was waiting for her with Star at the track opening.

"I'm sorry, but I'd better get out there. I'm already late for my workout," Christina said, turning away abruptly. "Why don't you come watch Star and see for yourself if he's a has-been or not?"

As Christina approached Dani, who was holding Star, she could feel her anger building. Her heart was pounding so loudly, she was sure anyone nearby could hear it. Her cheeks were hot, and she knew they were probably bright red. Somewhere in the back of her head an alarm was going off.

Go somewhere first and cool off! said a little voice.

Christina had been around horses long enough to know that she should never get near one when her temper was flaring. Always sensitive creatures, Thoroughbreds were particularly tuned to their riders' moods. And Star was especially sensitive. He would react quickly to Christina's tension, and there was no telling what would happen.

But just then Christina was in no frame of mind to listen to reason. There was only one thing she wanted to do: take Star out on the track and show that annoying reporter that he was ready to make racing history at Churchill Downs in May!

2

"THANKS, DANI," CHRISTINA PRACTICALLY GROWLED AS she took the reins from the groom, who was standing with a restless Star at the opening by Whitebrook's training oval.

"Sure thing," Dani replied, and gave Christina a leg up. "Hey, what's up? You're trembling," she added, stepping back.

Christina turned her head and said nothing.

"Is your ankle hurting that badly? Maybe you shouldn't ride today."

"It's nothing," Christina replied shortly, placing the reins in her left hand and fastening the chin strap on her helmet with her other hand.

"Nothing?" Dani persisted. "Is that why you're giving

me the look of death? Hey, did I do something wrong?"

Christina shook her head. "No, it has nothing to do with you. Somebody got me a little worked up, that's all."

The groom glanced at the reporter, who had just taken a spot at the rail a few yards from where Maureen and Ian were watching the morning works. "Oh, I get it. The reporter," Dani said. "Don't tell me you're nervous about that!"

Christina shook her head. "Who's nervous?" she said, her voice sounding brittle even to herself. *Furious is more like it,* she added silently. *A "has-been." Right. I'll show you has-been!*

Christina took up the reins, and Dani let go. Star skittered sideways. Dani rushed to his side to take Star's reins again.

"Whoa, boy. Easy," Dani murmured. "That's funny. He was as gentle as a pussycat when I tacked him up just now."

Christina muttered, "Guess he's getting all full of himself now that he knows he's going to go out there and blow some doors off."

Dani gave Christina a searching look and continued holding the reins.

"I've got him," Christina said. When Dani didn't let go, she added, "I said I've got him now."

"Uh, I think there's something the matter with your bridle," Dani said, stepping closer to Star and peering at his cheekpiece. "No, it's okay. Maybe I should check your girth."

Christina was puzzled for a moment, until a thought occurred to her. The groom was stalling, pretending something was wrong with her equipment when she knew everything was just fine. She was doing it so Christina wouldn't ride off on Star while she was seething with anger. The thought made Christina even more furious.

"Dani, come on. I've got to get out there," she snapped impatiently. "Ian's waiting. I'm okay. Really."

Dani opened her mouth to say something, then closed it. Shrugging, she walked over to collect one of the colts that had just been ridden out of the opening. Star pawed the ground while Christina shakily adjusted her foot in the stirrup. As she bent over, he tossed his head sharply, nearly unseating her.

"Knock it off, will you?" she said severely.

Christina tried to convince herself that Star was merely impatient to be out on the track, but deep inside she knew that she was rattling him.

As soon as we get out there and run, everything will be fine, she told herself.

Glancing at the oval, she saw that several other horses were already out there. Kevin was on one of Whitebrook's oldest racehorses, Thunder Bones. Melanie was trotting on Image, and Naomi Traeger, a jockey who had just come back from the Florida races,

21

was doing a slow gallop on Dazzle, a three-year-old.

Glancing at Ian, Christina could see him motioning to the other riders.

He's going to have us race, Christina realized.

That was fine by her, Christina thought, jamming on her goggles. She wouldn't worry about conserving Star this time. She'd give that reporter a story! She gripped her reins more firmly than was necessary, and Star threw up his head in alarm.

Ian hurried over to her, his mouth set in a tight line. "Something wrong?" the trainer asked.

Christina shrugged, hoping the trainer wouldn't push her for details. All she wanted was to get out on the track and start galloping Star as fast as he could go. She was going to pass every horse out there—and for good measure, she'd win the mock race by at least six or seven lengths!

"Christina? You haven't answered me."

Ian's voice cut into her fantasy. Seeing that the trainer was scrutinizing her face, Christina shook her head. She knew she'd better get her anger under control and quickly, or reporter or no reporter, Ian MacLean would order her off the track until she got herself back together.

"Nothing's wrong," she said quickly. "Sorry. I was just distracted for a moment."

Still looking doubtfully at her, Ian explained that after a warm-up jog, he wanted Star to join the other horses at the quarter pole and run to the three-quarter pole.

"I want you to let him out some, but not all the way. Even though he's got an audience, I still don't want to overdo it today."

Christina hoped her face didn't betray the fact that she had no intention of following the trainer's instructions. She had held Star back long enough. Too long, as a matter of fact.

Christina jogged Star around the track, still seething. She didn't know if she had ever been angrier before. What nerve that woman had to say that Star was a has-been!

She hardly noticed the big chestnut colt zigzagging under her because she was so caught up in rerunning the reporter's words in her head: *You mean the* Kentucky *Derby, don't you?*

Glancing down at her reins, which were now slippery with sweat, Christina wiped her clammy hands on Star's mane. She shook her head, trying to force herself to focus.

Forget what the reporter said. Think about Star. Think about the work.

Christina trotted next to Melanie, who was on Image. The black filly had only recently started racing, but she was already making a name for herself. Still, talk about a bad actor! Image was feisty and had a reputation for being tough to handle. But the filly

23

was behaving well that morning. As Star moved erratically, lightly bumping Image's side, Melanie's eyebrows went up in surprise.

"Take it easy on me, Chris," Melanie moaned. "I'm so tired, I just want to climb off this horse right now and curl up in the hay to sleep. I don't need any fireworks."

Normally Christina would have had a quick, lighthearted retort for her cousin, but she was in no mood for jokes at the moment.

Star did a couple of stiff-legged crow hops, and Image took advantage of the situation, breaking stride and dancing sideways, flattening her ears and shaking her head threateningly at him.

"What's gotten into Star?" Melanie asked, settling the filly down again.

"Nothing," Christina said, then, as Star spun around and bumped into Image again, she rebuked the horse sharply: "Cut it out!"

"Hey," Melanie complained, "I finally get Image to behave, and now the model student is trying to get her in trouble again so she'll get detention."

"Ha ha," Christina muttered, moving ahead of the filly.

She tried not to hear when Melanie called after her, "Don't tell me they've been stablemates so long, they're swapping traits. She's good as gold now, and Star's picking up Image's bad habits."

"No bad habits. He just wants to run," Christina said aloud, though there was no way Melanie would be able to hear her.

"Cool it, big guy," Christina warned after they had warmed up at a jog. She walked Star up behind the other horses and riders, who were starting to form a line side by side. "We've got a race to run. And today I don't care what anyone says—I'm going to let you rip!"

As they approached, Star cut sideways again, and Christina had to bring her leg against his side to correct him. That merely made Star cut back in the opposite direction. Out of the corner of her eye Christina saw the reporter talking into her tape recorder.

Without thinking, Christina pulled back on the reins sharply, and Star exploded into a series of bucks. Christina struggled to control the colt as they approached the other horses. They took their place in line, and Star jostled Thunder Bones, who was on his right.

"Hey, watch it," Kevin yelped. "You almost clobbered my knee. Do you want to totally ruin my chances for a scholarship?" Kevin had just returned to exercise riding after a long hiatus due to a knee injury he'd gotten playing soccer. He was counting on a soccer scholarship for college, and the last thing he needed was to reinjure his knee.

"Sorry," Christina said guiltily. She gritted her teeth and leaned over Star's neck as close as she could get, her eyes never leaving the stretch of track between his ears. "Let's show that so-called reporter just what you've got," she whispered to her horse.

Star tossed his head again and whinnied. At least he was standing still and not bumping the horses next to him. Christina waited for Ian's signal, wishing he would hurry. She wasn't sure she could hold Star much longer.

"Calm down," she commanded both herself and Star, but it didn't do any good.

At the precise second the trainer's hand fell, Christina gave Star more rein. Instantly Star leaped forward, throwing Christina off balance. Quickly she regained her seat and balanced herself over his shoulders. Star galloped on, stretching his neck out with the effort.

"Come on, boy!" she shouted, the wind whipping her face.

Dazzle and Image had gotten off to a good start, and Christina could see them pulling ahead of her. Thunder Bones always broke slowly, but when she glanced under her arm she found he was only a stride or two behind.

Christina wasn't concerned. That was how Star ran. He stayed back behind the leaders, and when the time came he'd make a run for it, leaving them all in the dust.

The key in the meantime, Christina knew, was to keep Star moving straight ahead. But she could feel her hands trembling. Star veered wide, cutting away from the rail. Kevin shouted something, and Christina pulled back quickly, just avoiding a collision with Thunder Bones's massive body.

She regrouped and started urging Star forward again, but he didn't respond. Christina knew it was because she kept sending him mixed signals—pulling with her hands and urging him on with her body. Taking a deep breath, she tried to force her hands to be quiet, but it was no use. Her heart was pounding and the adrenaline was pumping.

She squeezed her knees into Star's sides. They were coming up between Image and Dazzle, who were so close to each other, they seemed like one horse.

Take him wide and move around them. Christina could hear her mother's instruction echo through her brain as if Ashleigh were right there saying it.

Christina knew that going wide was the strategy she should take, but she didn't want to listen to reason; she wanted to win this race. And sometimes winning meant taking risks. She would cut between Image and Dazzle instead, even though it was the more dangerous option. Christina signaled Star to cut between Image and Dazzle.

But instead of moving forward, Star dropped back.

He's not paying attention to me!

Christina blinked as dirt started pelting her face and Star went back into zigzag mode.

Star's shutting me out—just like he did before I took him to Montana! Christina thought wildly

Star galloped halfheartedly on, his strides getting bunchier and choppier by the second. As Christina struggled with him, she tried desperately to remember what Lyssa had told her to do when Star stopped listening before.

Establish the connection so he'll follow the itancan, Lyssa had said. *Horses are herd creatures that are comfortable doing what the leader tells them to do—as long as they trust their leader. The hard part is establishing that trust and never breaking it.*

"Come on, boy," Christina yelled into Star's ear, but he ran as before, zigzagging from side to side and falling farther and farther behind the field. Thunder Bones passed them, and Star galloped on aimlessly, making no effort to chase him.

No matter what Christina did, it didn't make a difference. It was as if Star were riderless.

As they made the first turn, it occurred to Christina just what Lyssa would say if she were there right now: *The way you're riding right now, he is riderless. A horse can't follow a leader if there is no leader.*

Christina knew she had better start acting like a leader if she didn't want Star to look like a loser in front of the reporter.

Taking deep breaths to calm herself, Christina rode on, trying to throw off her anger and reconnect with

Star again. She focused on Thunder Bones's pumping hindquarters, driving Star toward them.

"Come on, boy, we can't let them get away," she cried.

But it was no good. The damage had been done. With every step they took, they fell farther and farther behind.

Christina knew that Star was running worse than he had the day he'd gotten sick at Belmont. That day, even though he was feeling terrible, he had run his heart out. Though the gap kept widening, Star had never given up. He had struggled on valiantly. But this time it felt as though he wasn't even trying!

Just then Star started moving up, and Christina felt her hopes rise as Star started gaining on Thunder Bones. But as he drew up beside the older horse, Star flattened his ears and snaked his head at his stablemate, gnashing his teeth angrily. Thunder Bones pulled ahead of him, and Star slowed down even more, as if glad to be rid of the competition even if it meant losing.

"Great," Christina muttered to herself. That reporter was getting the story she'd come for. Christina could see the headline as clearly as if it were puffed out in skywriting over Whitebrook: "Fallen Star: Bad Actor and Bad Runner!"

She had to do something—before it was too late!

3

"HURRY, STAR. WE CAN'T LOSE NOW!"

As the chestnut colt galloped erratically past the reporter, still trailing the others, Christina felt a fresh blast of fury course through her. This whole morning was turning out all wrong, and there didn't seem to be a thing she could do to stop it.

But she couldn't let that reporter go back and write a story about how poky Star was. She could just see Brad Townsend chuckling over his morning coffee about how clever he had been to unload Star before he went completely downhill.

Without thinking, Christina reached back and slapped Star on the flank with the palm of her hand. Star reacted violently. It was as if all his memories came back from the days when he'd been treated roughly by Ralph Dunkirk, the trainer at Townsend Acres. Then Star had acted out aggressively. Now he coiled his body in midflight and sprang sharply toward the rail, throwing Christina up onto his withers. She felt herself slipping and keeling to the outside as Star kicked into high gear and lurched forward, out of control.

Helplessly Christina clutched Star's neck and tried to hold on as he continued thundering down the track. Any minute, she feared, she would lose her grip and be thrown under those flying hooves. At any other time Star would have slowed when he felt Christina losing her grip. But this time he ran on without slowing.

And it's all my own stupid fault! she berated herself.

In spite of the incredible speed at which Christina was traveling, time seemed to stand still. Out of the corner of her eye she could see the ground rushing by. Suddenly she felt herself transported back to Montana, to the time when she had found herself hopelessly lost in the mountains while searching for Star, who had gotten loose. What had saved them then? Frantically Christina scanned her brain for the answer.

Lyssa's voice penetrated her consciousness: *You've got to join up. It's your only chance.*

Join up. Join up. The words pulsated through Christina in time to the beat of Star's hooves.

"Don't fight it. Join up," Christina whispered, willing herself to relax and stop the constant stream of angry messages she had been transmitting to Star from the moment she climbed into the saddle.

As Star slowed, Christina found it easier and easier to give in to his motion, though she was still clinging to the pommel of her saddle for dear life. With a huge effort she was able to gather the strength to right herself, and once more she was up in the middle of her saddle, perched over his shoulders.

"Oh, Star, I'm so sorry," she almost sobbed when Star finally came down to a jog.

Instantly Maureen was out on the track, her face white and her eyes wide. In the distance Christina could see Naomi, Kevin, and Melanie watching while they circled their horses back to meet her.

The enormity of what could have happened hit Christina all at once, and she slid off Star, her ankle giving way as she collapsed in the sand.

Expertly catching Star, Maureen called out, "Are you okay?" She crouched down and quickly checked the colt's legs to make sure he hadn't sustained any injury during his erratic run.

On her knees, Christina managed to nod.

Ian hurried over and helped her to her feet. "Are you hurt?"

Christina shook her head and took a few steps to prove she wasn't injured.

"I'm glad you're okay," the trainer said sternly.

"But that was about the worst example of horsemanship I think I've ever seen."

"I know," Christina whispered shakily. "It was totally my fault. I was angry, and Star just shut me out."

Ian brushed some dirt off her shoulder and said gruffly, "Next time you think twice before you climb aboard any horse while you're stewing about something. Got it?"

Christina hung her head, knowing she deserved every word the head trainer had said. She had never felt so frightened—or so stupid.

Limping off the track after Maureen had motioned that she'd lead Star over to Dani, Christina walked by the reporter, who was shutting off her recorder.

"What a shame," the reporter said, meeting Christina's eyes. "Dead last and unpredictable besides. You must be so disappointed."

She strode off to her car while Christina struggled to find a retort to such a ridiculous statement.

"I'm disappointed in me, but not in Star!" Christina shouted after her, though the reporter had already shut the door to her car and started up the engine.

While Christina changed for school, she thought about what the reporter would write. It definitely wasn't going to be complimentary, that much was certain.

"Oh, who cares what anyone else thinks!" Christina muttered as she grabbed her backpack and ran out to wait for her bus.

"Hey, Chris, have you heard *anything* I've said?"

Christina jerked herself out of her thoughts and focused on the face of her friend Katie Garrity, who was sitting next to her on the school bus that was rattling its way to Henry Clay High.

She wished Kevin could have driven her to school so that she wouldn't have had to make conversation, but his car was being repaired, so she and Melanie had had to take the dreaded bus.

What good does having a driver's license do me if I don't even have a car? Christina thought irritably.

Instantly she felt guilty that she was being such a grouch. Her friends had been so supportive throughout Star's illness. They didn't deserve to be ignored. "Sorry," she said brightly. "What did you say?"

Katie smiled. "Oh, it was no biggie. Don't tell me. You're worried about Star again, right?"

Lindsey Devereaux, who had been dating Kevin for a few months, added, "He isn't sick again, is he?"

Christina shook her head. "No. Star's fine. Something happened this morning, but it was my fault. Anyway, it's over now."

Melanie, who was sitting across the aisle, chimed

in. "*You* were almost over, you mean. Over and out."

Kevin leaned over the seat and added, "We all thought Christina was roadkill this morning."

"Stop exaggerating," Christina protested, playfully cuffing the top of Kevin's head. She just wished she could forget about the whole incident.

"What happened?" Katie asked. As usual, she wanted to hear every single detail. Melanie was only too happy to oblige.

Christina rolled her eyes as Melanie gave a play-by-play of that morning's race. When she finished, Katie whistled softly.

"My dad's always telling me never to get behind the wheel when I'm mad about something, but I never thought it applied to horses."

"It sure does," Christina muttered, embarrassed. Then she changed the subject. "So tell me, have you heard from any of the colleges you've applied to yet?"

She knew Katie had applied to some competitive East Coast colleges and was haunting the mailbox every day looking for a fat letter of acceptance.

Katie shook her head. "Not yet. I should have applied early admission somewhere. It's making me crazy."

Lindsey shrugged. "Let's just forget college for now and have fun while we're still in high school. Do you realize how quickly it'll all be over?"

"Not soon enough," Melanie griped.

Katie heaved a sigh. "No more homecomings, no more dances."

"No more equations. No more driver ed teachers. I won't miss it at all!" Melanie declared.

Katie turned to Christina. "How about you? Will you miss good old Henry Clay High when you're in college?"

Christina glanced at Melanie, silently reminding her not to spill the beans about her plans to put off going to college. She was going to tell all of her friends after she'd talked to her parents—and Parker.

"Miss Henry Clay High? A little. I'll miss my friends," Christina replied, although she knew she'd still see most of her buddies at the track or at horse-related events. It was amazing how horses kept everyone so tightly bound together.

"We won't ever lose touch," Katie promised as the bus turned into the high school's parking lot.

"We'd better not!" Christina said firmly. She resolved to put the terrible morning she'd had out of her head and just enjoy being with her friends, who were supportive of her no matter what.

After school, Christina had just changed and come down to the barn when she saw her mom and dad coming out of the barn office.

"What's this I hear about Star's disastrous work

36

this morning?" Ashleigh asked with concern. "We asked Ian about it, but he said it was better for us to hear it from you."

Christina's dad looked worried. "Is it true Star came in last? Is something wrong with him?" he asked anxiously.

Christina shook her head and sighed. "No, there's nothing wrong with Star," she said quickly.

"But he turned in the worst work he's ever had," Ashleigh pointed out. "And only two days after he had a great workout."

Christina sighed. "It wasn't Star's fault. It was completely and totally mine."

Christina's parents listened calmly while she explained everything. "You know how sensitive he is," she added. "I got all worked up by something that reporter said, and I couldn't shake it off."

"So you rode even though you were fighting mad," Ashleigh said, slowly comprehending. "You've been around horses ever since you were born. You know better than that. What were you thinking?"

Christina ducked her head.

"I guess no one needs to tell you what a big mistake that was," her dad added gently.

"I blew it," Christina muttered, wishing her parents would skip the lecture. She already knew how dumb she'd been.

"Well, luckily, no one was hurt, but that reporter

will certainly have a story," Ashleigh sighed.

"Fine with me," Christina replied, a slow smile spreading on her face. "I hope she splashes it all over the place that Star can't run worth beans anymore."

Christina's parents looked at her in surprise. "What do you mean?" her father asked.

"Let the whole world think Star doesn't have it in him anymore," she said. She twirled a lock of her reddish brown hair. "I honestly don't care what anyone else thinks. I know Star is great. That's enough for me."

Ashleigh looked doubtful. "I thought you couldn't wait to let everyone in on Star's incredible return."

"Oh, they'll find out eventually," Christina replied. "But in the meantime, maybe the press will decide Star's not newsworthy, and they'll leave us alone. Honestly, I can do without those guys watching us and asking me all sorts of annoying questions."

"Well, if you really feel that way," Ashleigh said, sounding unconvinced, "that's fine with us."

"On another important note, this came in the mail today," Christina's dad said.

He handed her a thick envelope from the University of Kentucky. Christina's throat went dry as she took the envelope. She opened it and scanned the cover letter.

"'Congratulations, you have been selected for admission to the University of Kentucky,'" she read

38

aloud. With a sigh, Christina folded the paper and stuffed it back in the envelope.

"What's with the sigh?" her mom asked, studying her face. "I thought you'd be jumping up and down that you were accepted. Not that you couldn't have gotten in anywhere you applied. Your grades have always been excellent."

Christina looked first at her mom and then at her dad. "I know this is going to come as sort of a surprise, but I've been thinking about something," she said in a shaky voice. "You might not like it."

"We won't like what?" Mike asked.

Christina shook her head. "I don't want to go to college right now."

"You want to *skip* college?" Ashleigh gasped.

Christina said quickly, "Not skip. I want to go to college. Just not yet. I want to race first," she went on. "I'll call the university and see if I can put off my admission until next year."

Ashleigh looked stunned. "What?" she said, leaning against the wall by the barn office.

"People do it all the time," Christina said.

"We had no idea," her mom mumbled.

Mike ran his hand through his hair. "No, we didn't . . . " he said, his voice trailing off.

Their heads snapped up at the sound of an approaching tractor.

"Mr. Reese, George wants you over at the stallion

barn," Jonnie yelled out as he chugged past the barn with a load of manure. "Terminator just kicked out one of the walls."

"We'll continue this discussion later," Mike said. He took off to see how much damage the most troublesome horse at Whitebrook had done, and Christina turned to her mother.

"Mom, I know this is kind of sudden and all, but I really think it'll work out. The thing is, I just want to race now. I'll see how racing goes, then I'll go to college."

Ashleigh held up her hand. "Your dad's right. We'll talk about it later."

"Okay," Christina said. "Then let's talk about Star. I have to race him—and soon."

"We'll talk about that later, as well," Ashleigh said distractedly as the office phone rang. "That'll be the vet. Perfect Heart is about to foal, and she's got some funny symptoms I don't quite like."

Christina sighed. There were always problems on the farm that required Ashleigh's immediate attention. Would she ever be able to get her mom to find time to think about what was next for Star? Christina wondered as she headed to the tack room.

Cindy and her friend from the United Arab Emirates, Ben al-Rihani, were just stepping out of the tack room door.

What are those two up to? Christina thought. The handsome young man had a Thoroughbred operation in Dubai and had already made a trip to Lexington in January, ostensibly on a horse-buying trip. But he had left when Cindy had gone to New York, and Christina hadn't expected to see him again. Christina knew they were spending a lot of time at Tall Oaks, the farm where Image had come from, and that Ben was planning to buy the horse farm.

Not seeing Christina, Ben and Cindy walked down the aisle, their heads together as they talked. Christina could hear their laughter echo through the barn, and she wondered what was so funny.

It's about time Cindy laughed about something, Christina thought as she entered the tack room and stepped over a stack of burlap bags. Ever since Cindy had had to quit racing, she'd been more sour than usual. Christina generally made it a point to stay away from Cindy, never sure when she'd snap.

Picking up a grooming box, Christina wandered over to Star's stall. She would brush him thoroughly, she decided, and give him a massage. That was the least she could do after she had put the colt through such an ordeal that morning. She had to make it up to him and assure him she would never break the trust between them again.

"So you've decided to forgive me, huh?" Christina said as he whickered mightily and nudged her shoulder while she unfastened the stall guard.

Taking the colt out of his stall, Christina led him to

the crossties and proceeded to groom him from nose to tail. When she had finished going over his burnished coat with a soft body brush, she stepped back to admire him.

Filling with pride, Christina ran her hand across his silky mane, over his powerful, sloping shoulders, and down his legs with their massive cannon bones. She looked into Star's dark, liquid eyes as he tossed his finely shaped head. He was a once-in-a-lifetime horse. She was convinced of that. And she didn't care if her mom and dad doubted it for now.

Come Derby day in May, everyone in the racing world would see for themselves that Wonder's Star had it all—breeding, conformation, speed, and heart to spare! He was born and bred to be a champion, and that's just what he would be.

4

"WONDER'S STAR HAS FALLEN."

Christina read the headline of the *Racing Reporter* the following morning, then tossed the paper aside. "Unbelievable!" she said, furious.

Parker Townsend, her boyfriend, reached for the paper and scanned the story. "Whoa," he said after he read a few lines. "Harsh."

"Tell me about it," Christina grumbled. She grabbed the paper from him and, without reading the rest of the story, slapped it onto the seat next to her. She looked around the local coffee shop where Parker had taken her after she had finished up her morning rides. She had been looking forward to spending Saturday morning with Parker, and now her whole mood was ruined by what she had seen in the paper.

Parker reached for her hand and searched her face until she was looking into his expressive eyes. "Chris, don't let those idiots get to you," he advised. "From what you told me, it was just a blip. You lost your cool, and Star freaked out a little. We all know Star's got talent, and so do you. Who cares what some hack journalist thinks?"

"Not just what she thinks, but everyone else. I told my parents I thought it was a good idea if the press blasted Star—that way they'd leave us alone. But it's another thing to see it in print like that."

"Like they say, don't believe everything you read," Parker said, squeezing her hand. "Anyway, no one reads the *Racing Reporter*."

"I hope not," Christina snorted, crumpling the straw from the glass of milk she had ordered.

"You know better than anyone that what she wrote about Star isn't true, so don't let it bother you. You've got more important things to think about, like whether to have chocolate chip pancakes or strawberry pancakes for breakfast."

Christina smiled in spite of herself. Parker always had a way of lifting her out of her bad moods. She looked over the menu and decided on the strawberry pancakes. Most jockeys on the taller side, like Christina, had to watch everything they ate so that they could make weight. She was lucky enough to be small-boned. What's more, her hectic schedule of riding, helping out in the barn, and going to school made it easy for her to remain slender.

"Now tell me what's new with you and Foxy," Christina said after they had ordered and the waitress had disappeared.

Parker and his mare, Foxglove, were on their way to competing in the Olympics for the U.S. three-day team. Over the last few months he had been training diligently with Samantha Nelson at her farm, Whisperwood, which was just down the road from Whitebrook. Christina was always eager to hear about his progress.

Parker blew the paper off his straw and stuck it in his glass of orange juice. "Well, Foxy's going really well," he said. "Sam's incredibly pleased at how much headway we're making in our dressage. And Foxy's jumping everything like a champ."

"That's great," Christina said. She knew how hard Parker had been working with his horse as well as keeping up with his studies at the University of Kentucky. It was a strict schedule, and combined with Christina's own rigorous schedule it didn't leave them much time to be together.

"Foxy and I have to be in top form. We're up against some serious competition," Parker added.

Competition like Lyssa Hynde and Soldier Blue! Christina thought. She had first met Lyssa when the girl competed against Parker at an important horse trial a few months before. Lyssa had blown everyone away with her easygoing riding style and unusual training methods.

Parker ran his hand through his dark hair and continued. "We built a couple of new cross-country jumps over at Whisperwood to keep Foxy on her toes. She was getting bored with the jumps we already had. I'm going to take her over them for the first time this afternoon. Should be interesting."

Earlier in her riding career, Christina had competed in combined training, too, and had trained her horse, Sterling Dream, in show jumping, cross-country, and dressage. But a few years ago she had been bitten by the racing bug and had reluctantly sold Sterling to Sam. She knew the mare had one of the best homes a horse could have, but she still missed Sterling and the sport she had once loved. She never tired of hearing about Parker's adventures at three-day events.

"What do the jumps look like?" she asked, leaning forward in interest. The crazy jumps that eventers had to jump over on a cross-country course always fascinated her.

Parker grinned. "Well, one looks just like a silver catering truck. It's got aluminum sides with red writing all over it. Foxy's eyes will bug out when she sees it, but I don't expect her to have any trouble jumping it."

"Foxy's braver than I am," Christina said, laughing.

"The other fence isn't so unusual—your basic poles-and-barrels job—but it really tests a horse's agility. You can't make any mistakes."

While Parker talked about the cross-country jumps and his training program, Christina watched his face. Although he was enthusiastic as ever, she thought she detected a shadow of concern steal over his eyes when he touched on the subject of the Olympics. But he didn't mention that anything was bothering him, and when their food arrived, Parker demolished his breakfast quickly and didn't expand on the subject.

He wouldn't have had that much of an appetite if some-thing was really worrying him, Christina thought after he dropped her off at Whitebrook later that morning. *I must have been projecting my own worries onto him,* she decided, waving as he drove off in his pickup truck. She watched the truck all the way to the road and remembered that once again she had forgotten to mention to Parker her plans to put off going to college.

What was holding her back from telling Parker? she wondered, then promptly forgot about it as the sweet scent of horses wafted up from the barn.

Turning, Christina ambled past the comfortable farmhouse and headed down the path that led to the barn.

Dani was the first one to approach her as she stepped into the dimly lit interior of the training barn. The groom was frowning as she thrust the *Racing Reporter* under Christina's nose.

"Did you see this garbage?" she demanded.

Christina winced a little at the sight of the offending headline. "Yeah," she said quietly.

"Aren't you going to call the editorial offices and demand a retraction?" Dani asked, her face like a thundercloud.

"How can I demand a retraction?" Christina replied, shrugging. "The reporter only wrote what she saw. I didn't display Star in his best light yesterday, that's for sure."

"Hmpf," sniffed the groom. "So maybe he didn't run his best time ever, but does that mean his only chance for greatness is to go to stud? The reporter said you have delusions of grandeur."

"Huh?" Christina said, grabbing the paper. She had only read the headline before. Obviously, she had missed the worst of the story. She walked to an overturned bucket and sat down to read. When she finished, she looked up at Dani, who was watching her with her arms crossed, frowning.

"Garbage is right," she said hotly. "I only read the headline before. That was bad enough. But the rest of the article is even worse. 'Now that his racing days

48

are behind him, we hope that Star can still fulfill his early promise through a successful career at stud. Maybe the next rising star will be one of his well-bred offspring, a youngster who can carry the dream all the way to the Derby finish line.'"

"How stupid," said Dani, grabbing a wheelbarrow and heading off toward the yearling barn. "Don't throw the paper away, though. I'll use it to line my parakeet's cage tonight," she yelled over her shoulder.

Christina smiled at Dani's loyalty. Walking by the barn office, she tossed the paper on her mom's desk and made her way back to Star's stall, trying not to let the article get under her skin any more than it already had.

"Put him out to stud? Please!" she muttered to herself. *Star's only three. He's got tons more races left in him! Stupid reporters!*

Jonnie stepped out of Star's stall as she approached. "I just fixed his automatic waterer," he said. "This horse of yours has been playing with it again. I think you need to work him harder—he has too much energy to spend making work for me."

Christina wasn't fooled a bit by the groom's tone. She saw the twinkle in his eyes. She knew Jonnie loved the playful colt almost as much as she did. "I'll be sure to talk to him about his behavior," she joked.

Jonnie chuckled. Then he said in a more serious tone, "I heard about the article that was written about him. Don't you believe a word of it."

Christina nodded. "Oh, I won't," she assured the groom.

Stepping into Star's stall, she stroked his velvety muzzle and slipped him some carrot chunks she'd saved for him. "And don't you believe anything, either," she whispered to her colt. "We've got some roses to win first, don't we, boy?"

Star snorted, sending a carrot shower onto Christina's sweater. "You big goof," she chided him. "Get serious, will you? We have lots of work to do between then and now."

The big colt tossed his head up and down as if in agreement, and Christina was momentarily cheered.

That evening Christina had just passed a bowl of mashed potatoes to her mom when the subject of the article came up.

"I'm sure you're not the least bit surprised, but everyone in town was talking about Star today," her father began conversationally. He had driven into Lexington earlier to pick up wood to repair Terminator's stall. "At the hardware store they were talking about how we were planning to enter him in the Kentucky Derby despite all he's been through." Mike Reese raise his eyebrows at his daughter skeptically.

"I still can't quite believe you said that."

"I believe it!" Christina shot back.

Ashleigh darted a glance at Christina before saying dryly, "I used to think no one read the *Racing Reporter*. Guess I thought wrong."

Mike nodded. "If there's bad news, people can't wait to get their hands on it. So many people stopped me to ask about Star, I ended up forgetting half the things on my list."

Christina stuck her fork into her potatoes and twirled it idly. "What were they saying?" she asked, though she already knew the answer.

"Well, the old guy who owns the store clapped me on the shoulder and told me how sorry he was. He said"—Christina's dad lowered his voice in imitation—"'Horses are heartbreakers. That's why I went into hardware instead.'"

Christina smiled at her dad's impression.

"Chuck at the bank wanted me to let him know when his cousin could book some mares."

"What did you say?" Ashleigh asked, eyes wide.

Mike grinned. "I said that Star was too young to be a daddy and that we'd let him know down the road."

Christina scowled. The jokes were starting to bother her. "I don't see how people can just make up their mind's that Star is washed up," she muttered. "I mean, he hasn't raced in ages. How can anyone know anything?"

Ashleigh looked at Christina. "Weren't you the one who said it was a good idea to let everyone think just that?"

Mike added, "I seem to remember you thought the press would leave you alone if they believed there was no more story when it came to Star."

"I *did* say that," Christina admitted. "And I guess I still believe it, but I don't want anyone looking at Star and feeling sorry for him or thinking bad things about him."

Ashleigh reached for the pepper shaker. "Well, you can't have it both ways," she said calmly. "Either you try to convince everyone that Star's on his way, or you let it rest and let them find out for themselves. I happen to think we're better off surprising them all at his next race."

"When *is* his next race?" Christina asked eagerly.

Ashleigh pursed her lips. "I've been considering a few, but right now I'm just not sure. Let's wait until he turns in another good work."

No matter how hard Christina pressed, that was the only answer Ashleigh would give. Christina felt more frustrated than ever, but she kept quiet about it.

From time to time during the meal Christina could see her dad's eyes wander over to the University of Kentucky envelope that was on the counter.

After dinner, much as she hated to, Christina brought up the subject of college once again.

"I know you guys are disappointed that I want to defer my admission," she said. "But honestly, I've given it a lot of thought. I can pick right up the September after this one, and it won't make any difference."

Mike looked at her thoughtfully, stroking his chin. "Once you take time off, it's harder to go back to school."

"It won't be for me," Christina said adamantly. "I've always studied hard, and this way I'll have more independence and responsibility to bring to my college experience."

Pleadingly she looked at her mother. "Racing is all I want to do," she added. "If I don't go for it now, I might never have a chance to race again."

Ashleigh looked at Christina's dad, and Christina could see in their faces that they were giving in.

"Oh, well, what's one year?" Ashleigh said slowly.

Christina jumped up and hugged both her parents. "I promise. It'll be okay."

Now to break the news to Parker, she thought as she climbed the stairs to her room.

Christina was sitting at her desk trying to make headway on an English essay that was due next week when the phone rang.

"Hello?"

It was Parker. "Hi, Christina," he said. His voice sounded cold, as if he was angry at her about something.

Christina gripped the phone. "What's up?" she asked, trying to sound casual.

"Oh, nothing. It's just that I heard some news from Melanie today, and I kind of wondered why my girlfriend didn't tell me herself."

Christina winced at the way he emphasized the word *girlfriend*.

"You mean about my not going to college," she said slowly, her shoulders slumping.

"Well, yeah, that little detail," Parker replied sarcastically. "So when were you going to fill me in?"

"I—I meant to," Christina said. "But I was kind of distracted by everything, and anyway, you seemed to have something on your mind. Oh, I don't know. . . ." Her voice trailed off weakly.

"I thought you were applying to the University of Kentucky," Parker accused.

"I did, and I got accepted, but I've changed my mind. I want to take the year off and be with the horses," Christina said. She toyed with the phone cord.

"You know, it's not easy being out in the world with only a high-school diploma," Parker said. "Do you really want to struggle all your life the way your parents have?"

Christina could hardly believe her ears. Since when did Parker have the right to judge her parents? She had always thought he admired the way they had built Whitebrook from nothing. Sitting upright on her bed, she said, "Two things. I *am* planning to go to college. I'm just waiting for a year, that's all. And second, I happen to be proud of the way my parents have worked hard for what they have, Parker."

She almost added, *I hear your snob genes coming through*. But having learned her lesson from this morning about plunging on when she was angry, she bit back her words. She had enough on her mind without getting into a huge fight with her boyfriend.

"I didn't mean that the way it sounded," Parker said quickly. "I just don't want to see you make a big mistake."

"I don't happen to think it's a big mistake. But I *am* sorry you had to hear about it from someone else," Christina said, forcing herself to remain calm.

"Yeah, well, I guess I shouldn't have dumped on you about it," Parker said in what sounded to Christina like an apology. "Anyway, guess who ended up at urgent care today?"

"Who?"

"Me!"

"What happened?" Christina gasped.

"Don't worry. I got a painkiller, and it doesn't hurt anymore," Parker said.

Christina stood up, alarmed. "What doesn't hurt anymore? What happened, Parker?"

"Well, remember that catering-truck jump I told you about?" Parker asked.

"What about it?"

"Let's just say that Foxy went over it, but I kissed it," Parker said.

It took a few minutes for Parker to fill Christina in. When they had gotten to the jump, the sun had caught it just right, and the glare reflected back into his eyes. Foxy had been feeling fresh and jumped it with room to spare, but, Parker explained, he had lost his balance and fallen off.

"I managed to find the only sharp piece I forgot to hammer down, and I cut up my arm pretty good. But luckily it was only a few stitches. And thank goodness Foxy and the other horses didn't get cut."

Concern for the horses always came first with Parker, Christina knew, but she was relieved that the accident hadn't been more serious.

"The irritating part was waiting forever in the urgent-care center," Parker grumbled. "And they didn't even have any good horse magazines to kill the time. I've been in a pretty bad mood since."

"Well, I guess we both had crummy days," Christina said. The thought occurred to her that Parker probably wouldn't have been so mad at finding out about her college plans if he hadn't already been set off by his fall.

"How was your day crummy?" Parker asked. "Don't tell me you're still dwelling on that article in the *Racing Reporter*."

"Well, yeah," Christina confessed. "Even if I don't believe a word of it, it really bothers me. My dad said everyone in town was talking about it today."

Parker laughed. "I hope you're just not thinking of the public relations aspect of this," he said.

Christina was mystified. "What does public relations have to do with it?"

"Plenty. You know as well as I do that people love Cinderella stories. When they see that 'poor old has-been' out on the racetrack setting records, they'll be falling all over themselves with excitement. You'll see some very different headlines."

Parker just might be right, Christina thought after they had hung up. She chewed the end of her pencil and looked out her window at the clouds covering the moon.

But then she glanced at a curled photo jammed in the corner of her dresser mirror. It was a picture of herself astride Star in the winner's circle just after she'd won the Laurel Stakes. She was holding a huge, gleaming cup, and Star was standing proudly like a statue. She studied it for a long time before turning back to her English paper.

5

"OKAY, CHRIS, YOU KNOW WHAT TO DO," ASHLEIGH CALLED, glancing at her stopwatch. "Let's breeze him. I want to clock him today."

It was Monday morning, and Christina and Star were on the training oval. They had just finished cantering once around the track clockwise to warm up. It was a cool, windy day, and Christina could tell Star was feeling good. His ears were pricked sharply forward, and his nostrils were flared. At the starting line he arched his neck and snorted, impatient to be off. At Ashleigh's signal, Christina let Star break away.

Star leaped forward, accelerating with each stride. Christina followed her colt's surging motion with her body, balancing lightly in the tiny saddle on his back. She guided Star toward the rail, and they swept around the turn. Christina saw the three-quarter pole just ahead, and she eased her grip on Star's reins slightly. Star lengthened his stride in response. The wind whipped Christina's face as the big colt thundered down the track, flying past each pole. Concentrating for all she was worth, Christina kept her gaze fixed ahead.

Heading down the backstretch, Star thrust his head forward and almost pulled the reins through Christina's fingers. His shoulders were pumping as he shot out even faster. The dirt clods flew fast and furious behind them.

Christina knew that Star was setting fast fractions, and as the big chestnut sped past the black-and-white mile marker, she smiled happily. They were flying! For a few seconds she lost herself in the sensation of Star's pounding hooves and snorting breaths. Finally she stood up in her stirrups to ease him back down to a jog. Star shook his head against the pull on the reins, fighting to keep going.

"Easy, Star," Christina murmured. "Good boy."

Star broke into a jog, and Christina circled him until he slowed to a walk. He was barely even blowing. Christina knew he could have run another mile equally fast. She tried to suppress the huge smile that was spread across her face.

"Well, how did he do?" she called to her mother as she passed her on the rail.

Ashleigh was staring at her stopwatch with seem-

59

ing disbelief. "Wow," she said. "He hasn't clocked a time like this since before Belmont."

Christina didn't wait to hear the time. She trotted on, cooling Star and finally taking him out through the gap. The exact time didn't matter to her. She knew Star had run well. And she knew he had it in him to do even better.

Well, it's now or never, Christina thought. This was the perfect opportunity to talk with her mom about letting Star go with the other Whitebrook horses to Florida.

After she cooled Star, Christina rode over to Ashleigh, who was writing notes on her clipboard.

"Star was pretty incredible, wasn't he?" Christina began.

Ashleigh nodded. "I was certainly impressed," she said.

"Impressed enough to let me take him to Florida?" Christina burst out.

Ashleigh turned to her. "What?"

"Florida. I think Star should go," Christina told her. "I want to run him in the Florida Derby. All the other good horses are running."

Ashleigh pursed her lips. "You're serious, aren't you?" she said softly.

Christina nodded. "You bet I am."

"Look," her mom said gently, "I won't argue that he just had a great work, but come on, Chris. There's no way he's ready for Florida. Those other horses have been racing fit all season."

Christina felt her cheeks heat up.

"Star's just run one of his fastest times ever, and you don't think he's ready?" Christina protested as she walked in small circles in front of Ashleigh. She lowered her voice as Melanie trotted past her on Image. "You're sending Image and some of the other horses down there. Why can't Star go?"

Ashleigh reached over the rail to pat Star's glistening neck. "I know it's hard to understand, considering how well he's running these days. But I'm just getting used to the idea that Star is ready to race at all, let alone think seriously about running him in a race like the Florida Derby. He's going so well now. Let's not take any risks with him, Chris."

"Star's tough enough to take it," Christina insisted. "He'll never go to the Kentucky Derby if we don't enter him in a single prep race."

"Prep race? Oh, Chris, you're not still dreaming about the Kentucky Derby for Star, are you?"

"Yes." Christina's eyes locked with her mom's. "I am."

Ashleigh looked away for a moment and was silent. Then she took a deep breath. "You do dream big, don't you?" she said, more to herself than to Christina.

"Why not?" Christina challenged. "Star's perfectly

healthy now, and he's getting more fit every day. And look at this workout. You said you were impressed. What more do you need? Why not let him prove himself in a race?"

Christina's mom tapped her clipboard with her pen, staring at Star's time where she had written it down.

"And if he's going to go to the Kentucky Derby, he's got to run in some of the prep races," Christina said.

Ashleigh looked up and cracked a fleeting grin. "Hate to remind you, but I *have* had a little experience with these things."

Christina flushed. She certainly hadn't forgotten that Ashleigh had won the Derby herself. But this was different—a different time, a different horse, and different circumstances. She had to make her mother see that.

Ashleigh held up her hand as Christina was about to speak again. "I'm thrilled that Star is running well, but it's way too soon for us to think about running him in the Kentucky Derby. He's still working his way back into top condition. He's just not there yet."

Christina frowned. "But he's in great condition. Look at him. He's hardly blowing or sweating—I mean, considering how fast he just ran."

"Speaking of which, since he's just run, he needs to walk out some more," said Ashleigh pointedly in a voice that indicated that the conversation was finished. She lifted her stopwatch and gave Naomi the signal to start her gallop on Fast Gun.

Christina wanted to keep insisting, but she knew it was a losing battle. Her mother could be awfully stubborn sometimes. She resisted the urge to glare at her mom while she finished cooling Star and handed him to a waiting Dani.

She had just finished putting away her tack after exercising the other horses she had been assigned when Naomi came into the tack room.

"Star's looking good," the jockey said cheerfully as she placed her light saddle on the rack.

"Thanks," Christina replied. "I wish *other* people would see that."

Naomi picked up some neat's-foot oil and a bar of saddle soap. "I hear you aren't going to Florida," she said. "But I hope you're not too discouraged. There'll be other races."

Christina snorted. "Yeah. I just hope they're not too late to make a difference." Her eyes filled with tears, but she brushed them away quickly. She didn't want everyone to know how upset she was.

Naomi stopped for a moment at the tack room door. "I've seen horses who've been brought back too quickly. It isn't pretty."

"I know, I know," Christina said.

She stood for a moment after Naomi had left, considering her words, and decided the jockey was way wrong. No one knew Star like she did—that was the trouble.

As she hurried up to the house to change for school, it occurred to her how closed-minded people were. Once they had decided that a horse was finished, that was that. They wouldn't even consider that maybe things could change and get better, that a horse who had run into trouble could get back in the game again.

"My own mom won't even see it my way," Christina complained to Melanie as they clambered aboard the bus a few minutes later. "I just don't get it. Star's doing so well."

"Your mom has her reasons, I guess," Melanie said neutrally.

"Yeah, maybe," Christina muttered.

Melanie fiddled with a strap on her backpack. "You have to admit it takes some getting used to—one minute Star's almost dying, then the next thing you know you're talking about running him in the Kentucky Derby. It's just hard to believe he's back and running as fast as he used to run."

"Well, he is. Maybe even faster. And he's ready for Florida. I don't see why Mom won't let us go," Christina moaned. "I can't stand it. You'll be at Gulfstream, and I'll be stuck here."

Melanie eyed her for a moment as the bus rattled

along. "I wish you were coming. It'll be boring without you there."

When Melanie had come to live at Whitebrook from New York City a few years earlier, the two girls hadn't gotten along at first. Now they were best friends, having bonded through their shared love of horses.

Christina smiled. "You'll be too busy to be bored. You'll have your hands full with Image down there. And you're riding other horses, too. You won't have time to miss anyone."

Melanie didn't say anything.

"And isn't Jazz coming to watch Image? I'm sure you'll be extra busy," Christina added.

Melanie shrugged. "So what if he's coming? Just like you said, I'll be too busy to notice. Anyway, back to your problem. Are you sure you can't talk your mother into letting you go? After all, you can be pretty persuasive when you want to be."

"I've been working on her for days," Christina replied. "She won't budge."

Melanie twisted a hank of her blond hair and raised an eyebrow. "Well, it seems to me that you've been in this situation before, and you managed to handle it yourself."

Christina was mystified. "What are you talking about?"

"How about the time when your parents didn't

want you to test for your apprentice license and you sneaked out and rode Sassy?"

"What does that have to do with this?" Christina demanded.

Melanie shrugged. "Just that when you set your mind to something, you usually figure out a way to get it done, that's all."

"This is different."

"Well, maybe. Maybe this time your mom's right. After all, Star was incredibly sick," Melanie said resignedly.

Some friend you are, Christina thought irritatedly, turning away from her cousin. She knew she was being unfair. She shouldn't blame Melanie for not being able to come up with a solution to her problem.

That morning Christina tried to concentrate in her classes, but her mind kept drifting to Star. No matter how much she thought about it all, she couldn't figure out how to persuade her mom to see things differently. By lunchtime she felt so low, she could hardly eat. It didn't help when she overheard Melanie at the next table telling someone else about how warm she'd heard it was in Florida. She was glad that Melanie had to stay after school for math tutoring, so she wouldn't have to hear any more about Florida on the bus ride home.

After the bus dropped her off at Whitebrook, Christina made her way to her room, dumping her books and changing into her barn clothes. Then she headed for the kitchen.

She had just found a leftover blueberry muffin from breakfast for a snack when her mom came in through the back door holding a stack of old *Bloodhorse* magazines.

"I can't believe the clutter that builds up in the barn office," Ashleigh said brightly, setting the stack on the small table by the door. "After dinner I'm going to go through these and get rid of as many as I can."

Christina knew her mom was aware of the tension between them and was making small talk as a way to avoid bringing up the sore subject of Florida. She bit into her muffin so that she wouldn't have to say anything.

"Where's Melanie?" Ashleigh asked, looking around.

"She stayed after school for math tutoring," Christina explained. "She said someone was giving her a ride home."

"Well, I'm glad she's getting some help," Ashleigh said. "I'm still not sure she should be missing school to go to Florida, not when she's struggling with some of her subjects."

At the mention of the word *Florida*, Christina

wanted to choke. She swallowed her bite of muffin, then wrapped up the rest in a napkin.

Ashleigh placed her hand on Christina's shoulder, and Christina resisted the urge to squirm away. "Look," her mom said gently, "I know it's hard for you to understand, but Ian and I agree that Star's not ready for Florida."

Christina lifted her eyes to meet her mother's. "You're just like that reporter. You don't think Star's good enough for the Derby, do you? You think he's a has-been."

Ashleigh shook her head. "You're wrong about that. I must admit I didn't dare think about it until I saw his workout this morning. But it's late in the game. The Derby's coming up so soon, and we can't afford to make any missteps. That's why we have to strategize extra carefully."

Christina wasn't convinced. "Keeping Star at home doesn't sound like a strategy to me."

Ashleigh regarded her for a moment before she said, "I didn't say Star had to stay at home. I just said that maybe Florida isn't the place for him right now."

Whatever that means, Christina thought gloomily as the phone rang. Her mother answered it, and Christina headed to the barn to complain to Star.

The colt appeared more interested in the carrot Christina had tucked in her back pocket than in the details of her argument with her mother.

"Oh, Star. What are we going to do?" Christina asked, stroking Star's velvety nose as he crunched his carrot.

She stood next to her horse, lost in thought. Maybe Melanie was right. Maybe she needed to take matters into her own hands. *I could talk Parker into trailering Star to Turfway. I could enter Star in some small race and—* But as quickly as she came up with the idea, she dismissed it. Simply running in a race wasn't the point. The key was to enter Star in a serious race, so everyone would begin to take *him* seriously.

As far as Christina was concerned, that meant Florida, where all the other Derby contenders were running—Brad Townsend's beloved Celtic Mist, for one.

"Don't worry, Star," Christina sighed. "I'll think of something."

She hoped she sounded more convincing than she felt.

6

"WHOO-HOO!"

Two days later, Christina raised a fist and punched the air in a gesture of triumph as Wonder's Star passed the mile marker. She'd watched the poles as Star galloped past them, and she knew that Star had just finished an even faster workout than the one he'd put in on Monday. One look at Ian McLean's astonished face confirmed her feeling. He blinked as he checked his stopwatch again and gave her a thumbs-up gesture.

"Star, you're the best," Christina said, standing in her stirrups and rocking her weight back as she started to slow the powerful colt. As usual, Star pulled at his bit, eager to keep going. "Not just now," Christina crooned. "Save some of that for your next race."

She held Star in as a couple of horses galloped by him along the rail. Her heart pounding from the workout, Christina took big gulps of the cold March air while she continued to steady the prancing colt.

"Wasn't he incredible?" she asked the head trainer as she took Star off the track.

"Not bad," Ian grunted, but his eyes showed that he was ecstatic.

"Did we set a record?" Christina asked while sliding off Star's back.

"Pretty nearly. Great fractions, anyway. Too bad your mom is in Lexington today. She'd have liked to see this."

Christina nodded. "Yeah, she would have." *And maybe it would have made her change her mind*, she thought.

The trainer turned his attention back to Kevin, who was breezing Igor. Christina pulled off Star's sweaty saddle, handing it to Jonnie. It was Dani's day off, so Christina would be the one to cool Star out and rub him down. She patted his sweat-soaked neck and told him how wonderful he was all the way to the wash stall.

"Wait till Mom hears about this work," she said happily, reaching up to scratch Star under his jaw. "She'll be so excited."

But when she heard the roar of the van backing up into the stable area, her happiness over how fast Star's work had been began to ebb. This was the day that several Whitebrook horses, including Image, were to leave for Gulfstream.

Star should be on that van, Christina thought. If only he'd turned in the time he'd clocked that morning a few days earlier. Surely that would have convinced her parents that Star was ready to go.

But by the time Star was walked out and cooled, she decided that it probably wouldn't have made a difference. Her mom's mind was made up, and that was that.

Christina tried to shut out the sounds of horses being loaded as she bathed Star, but it was no use. Her dad's voice as he called out instructions and Melanie's laughter carried into the wash area, drilling into her the fact that she and Star were being left behind. She felt her spirits swirl to her feet and cascade down the drain along with the dirty water.

After bathing Star, Christina led him down the barn aisle. In the distance she could see Jonnie and Joe loading the equipment. Pausing for a moment, Christina shielded her eyes from the morning sun as she watched Melanie lead Image up the ramp. Star nickered at his stablemate, and Image responded with a long, shuddering whinny.

A lump rose in Christina's throat, and she turned away. *It's so unfair!*

Leading Star to his stall, Christina saw her dad

come down the aisle toward her. She opened the stall door and Star stepped in, up to his knees in deep bedding.

"Well, we're off to Florida, Chris," Mike said to Christina from outside Star's stall. He blew her a kiss.

Christina plastered a smile on her face. "Good luck," she said, unable to hide the envy that crept into her voice.

"Don't be too disappointed, kiddo," her dad added. "I know this is rough for you, but believe me, it's for the best. Your mom's just waiting for the right time and the right race for Star. We want him to go to the Derby as much as you do."

Then take us with you, Dad! she wanted to yell. Instead she said, "Have a safe drive."

She watched him go, tears threatening to spill down her cheeks. Just then she felt Star's whiskery lips reach over to tickle her ear, and she cracked a smile.

"Oh, you're right, big guy," she told Star firmly as she dried him off with a fluffy towel. "Not going to Florida isn't the worst thing in the world."

Yes, but sitting around waiting for Mom to decide you're ready to race again is, she thought, her smile fading once more.

After school that afternoon Christina headed for the barn. With Naomi and Melanie gone, there was more work spread among fewer people. She checked several broodmares who were ready to drop their foals any day, helped Jonnie bring in a couple of yearlings from the paddocks, and started filling buckets with feed.

As the sun started to set and Christina moved from stall to stall carrying feed buckets, the frustration she had felt all day rose to the surface. Image's stall was empty, and so were Fast Gun's and Rascal's. The empty stalls were simply another reminder that she and Star were stuck at home while others were headed toward their dreams.

She filled a bucket with grain, vitamins, and supplements, then went into Star's stall. Star plunged his nose into his feed, and Christina watched him quietly for a few moments. Then, securing his blanket, she finished up her chores and headed to the house to help with dinner.

Ashleigh was humming under her breath as she pulled out a steaming broccoli-cheese casserole.

How can Mom be so calm when I'm so frustrated? Christina wondered, pulling out the silverware and setting the plates on the table. *She forgets what it was like when she believed in Wonder and everyone else was holding her back.*

"So how was school today?" Ashleigh asked, placing the casserole on the counter.

School? Who cares about school? "Oh, it's all right,"

Christina said. "We finished reading *The Grapes of Wrath*. I have to write an essay on it tonight."

"That's nice," her mom said, spooning up the casserole.

Christina switched the subject abruptly. "Did Ian tell you about Star's great work this morning?"

Ashleigh nodded. "Yes. He just keeps outdoing himself. As a matter of fact—"

Just then the phone rang, and Christina's mother answered it. "Oh, hello, Rich." It was the farm's accountant, and Ashleigh's face clouded over as she listened.

"Yes, of course. Let me go down to the office and find that file for you," she said.

She put her hand over the receiver and mouthed, "Ugh—taxes." She motioned for Christina to keep eating while she went down to the barn office to check up on some numbers.

Christina ate a few bites of her dinner, wondering what her mom had been about to say about Star. She waited for a while, but Ashleigh didn't return. Christina finished her dinner alone and went up to her room.

With a sigh, Christina pulled out her homework. Scowling, she tried to write her English essay, but her mind kept wandering. Soon she found herself doodling in the margins, and after an hour she gave up. It was no use. She'd have to write it the next day during lunch. Shoving her papers and books aside, she sat idly at her desk, drumming her fingers along the edge.

After a while she decided to call Parker. He could always cheer her up. But then she remembered his reaction about her college plans. The last thing she wanted was to get into a discussion about that again. She had enough on her mind.

Reluctantly she set down the receiver and stood up.

Inspiration—that was what she needed. And she knew just where to find it.

Slipping downstairs, Christina wandered into the den. Combing through the stacks of videos, she finally found the one she was looking for. It was a professionally made video of Wonder's win in the Kentucky Derby many years ago. Now slightly scratchy and inclined to jump around on the screen, it still gave Christina the shivers when she watched it.

She had seen it many times, of course, but somehow this time it seemed brand-new. Christina settled into the comfy old couch and felt the hair stand up at the back of her neck as the soft strains of "My Old Kentucky Home" filled the small room. The camera panned over the famous twin spires, then zoomed down to the crowd pouring through the admissions gates.

Christina ignored the credits rolling past and instead focused on the montage of elegantly dressed

76

people holding racing forms, mint julep glasses, and binoculars. They were filling the grandstands and swarming through the infield. The announcer's voice rolled smoothly, explaining the history of the famous race and describing the winners who had gone on to win the acclaimed Triple Crown.

For a few delicious seconds Christina imagined what it would be like to add Star's name to that list. Soon her attention was riveted on the well-bred horses being paraded in front of the grandstand.

Her eyes went immediately to Jilly Gordon, mounted on Ashleigh's Wonder, who was prancing on her lead next to her escort pony. Christina's breath caught in her throat at the sight of Star's dam. A glowing copper chestnut, Wonder had a lovely, refined head, grandly sloping shoulders, and slender, powerful legs. She was beautiful, every inch a Thoroughbred. No wonder her mother had loved her so much. For the first time Christina could understand how Wonder's death had devastated her mom so much that she could hardly look at Star for the first few months of his life.

The camera focused on each horse for a few seconds, then pulled back so that the full field came into view. The other horses had been impressive, too. As the video swept over Wonder's fellow contenders, Christina could see just what competition Wonder had been up against. The only other horse Christina recognized was Townsend Prince. He, too, looked gorgeous and powerful.

When the camera cut to the horses being loaded into the starting gate, Christina leaned forward, holding her breath. She never tired of watching this race. It was as though she were there herself, in the chute, every muscle poised, waiting for the bell to sound and the gate to fly open.

"They're off!" the announcer's voice crackled.

A gray horse named Sandia had set a blistering pace. Christina could see that Jilly was holding Wonder to a comfortable third place, biding her time before she made her move. Christina smiled as Townsend Prince started gaining on Wonder. The colt's efforts had made Ashleigh nervous as she'd watched in the stands, but Christina knew the Townsend colt didn't have a chance against Wonder.

Wonder shot into first coming around the turn, and though Townsend Prince was gaining ground, he just didn't have it. Wonder surged forward and, against the odds, won the Kentucky Derby by a length.

A thrill shot through Christina as she watched her mom make her way to the winner's circle. As the roses were draped over Wonder's shoulders, Christina's eyes filled with tears, the way they always did when she watched this video.

That'll be Star, Christina thought. She stood up and

clicked off the video machine. Suddenly her mind started whirring as fast as the horses she'd just seen run in that long-ago race. Wonder never would have stood in that winner's circle if Ashleigh hadn't taken some risks. If she had played it safe and not pressed on when the going got tough, Wonder's name never would have been written into the annals of Derby history. But Ashleigh had ignored everyone's words of criticism and doubt and thrown her heart into making Wonder a winner.

So why was her mother being so cautious with Wonder's son? Wonder's blood ran through Star's veins. The same fire that had so brightly lit his dam from within burned in Star. Grabbing the clicker, Christina rewound the tape so she could watch the finish again.

Just then the phone rang again, but she made no move to pick it up. She heard her mom hurry into the kitchen to answer it.

Moments later Ashleigh walked into the room, holding a stack of racing schedules. "Oh, there you are," she said. "Did you have enough to eat?"

Turning on the light, she regarded Christina, then the screen. A small smile played across her face as she watched her beloved Wonder toss her head and prick her ears proudly for the win photos at the Kentucky Derby. Then she seemed to snap out of her trance.

"That was your dad on the phone," she told

Christina. "He says everything's going well and that the horses are traveling well. Melanie says hello."

When Christina didn't answer, she added, "Why are you watching that old tape again? You've seen it a hundred times."

Christina bit her lip and nodded. Then she burst out, "I still can't believe you're being so unfair about Florida. You had your chance. Don't you want me to have mine?"

Ashleigh regarded her. "I'm sorry you feel that way," she replied. "I do want you to have your chance. And I understand how frustrated you must feel, Chris, but it's too soon for Star to be exposed to the rigors of races like the Florida Derby yet. The competition's just too much for him right now. It's too soon for him to face the horses that are down there."

"Like who?" Christina protested.

"Celtic Mist, for one," Ashleigh said.

"You don't think he can take on Celtic Mist after the way he ran this morning?" Christina sputtered.

Ashleigh grinned. "Oh, I'm confident he can beat him. The question is *when*. Timing is everything in racing, like it is with so many other things. And I just don't think the time is right now for Star to go head-to-head with the likes of Celtic Mist."

"How can you say that?" Christina cried.

"Christina," Ashleigh insisted, "I've been racing horses for quite a few years. Call it a gut feeling, call it instinct. I am confident that our Star will have his day, but only if we don't push him too quickly. You just have to trust me on this."

Christina felt her shoulders slump.

"But what I wanted to tell you before was that I did talk to Ian this afternoon about Star's work, and he reminded me of a track we might have over-looked—Fair Grounds Race Course in New Orleans. I was looking over the schedule, and there's a race or two that might be just right for Star."

Christina sat up. "New Orleans?" she said dubiously.

"Fair Grounds has the second-longest stretch in the country. That ought to be good for Star, since he tends to come from behind. He'll have plenty of room on that long stretch to make his move. And the competition won't be as tough, either. We'll see how he does in one of the smaller stakes races at Fair Grounds and go from there."

Smaller stakes races? Christina furrowed her brow. "But our van is at Gulfstream," she said, knowing she sounded like a brat. She couldn't help it. It was just so unexpected.

"I've got some friends who are vanning their horses down in a few days, and they said they had room for a few more. So I thought maybe we could take Dazzle and Rhapsody and see how they do in some of the other races."

When Christina made no reply, Ashleigh put her hands on her hips. "What's wrong? I thought you'd be thrilled to hear that Star is going to race again. Why the long face?"

Christina blew out a breath, making her bangs flutter. "I *am* happy, I guess. It just took me by surprise, that's all. I've never been to Fair Grounds."

"Well, here. Why don't you look through these?" Ashleigh tossed the Fair Grounds race schedules onto the coffee table. "I was thinking about one of the shorter races, nothing too difficult. Take a look. See what you think."

After her mom left the room, Christina sat on the sofa with her feet tucked under her, staring at the blank TV screen.

Fair Grounds instead of Gulfstream? A short, easy race instead of a tougher, more grueling prep race? *What good is that?* Christina thought with a snort. She'd be at some small track down in New Orleans while everyone else would be racing in the prestigious prep races in Florida.

Picking up a stack of racing schedules her mom had left behind, she riffled through them halfheartedly. None of the races looked exciting. Most of them were too short for Star, who definitely wasn't a sprinter. When it came to the longer races, Christina hardly recognized any of the horses that were entered. No doubt about it—the more serious Derby contenders were at Gulfstream. Her eyes traveled down the list and stopped when she saw a listing that made her face light up.

The Louisiana Derby. A grade-two, mile-and-a-sixteenth prep race, held in mid-March.

Christina scanned the page, smiling as she read the names of two past Louisiana Derby winners, Black Gold and Grindstone, who had gone on to win the Kentucky Derby.

"The Louisiana Derby is emerging as an important prep race for the Championship Series races," the description read. "Early nominations include acclaimed horses from across the United States." *And the purse would pay the farm's taxes and then some*, Christina thought. But even more important was that if Star won this race, he'd prove he had the stuff to run in the Kentucky Derby. Maybe her mom was right after all: Fair Grounds *was* perfect for Star.

There was just one problem. Her mother wanted to enter Star in a small stakes race. When Ashleigh had mentioned Fair Grounds, the Louisiana Derby wasn't what she'd had in mind.

But this time I'm not giving in, Christina thought, gearing up for another battle of wills.

7

THE NEXT MORNING CHRISTINA WAS UP WELL BEFORE dawn. She'd lain awake half the night thinking about what Melanie had said a couple of days earlier: *When you want something, I've always known you to make it happen.*

And then the plan had come to her.

Pulling on her oldest jeans and a worn sweatshirt, Christina shoved the rolled-up Fair Grounds race schedule into her back pocket. She slipped down to the kitchen, where she grabbed a wicker tray and opened a starched linen napkin that she set on the tray. Hurriedly she pulled out a plate, some silverware, and, as an afterthought, a dusty bud vase that had sat long forgotten under the sink. Frowning, she realized that there was nothing in the cupboard to cook her mother for breakfast. No pancake mix. No syrup. There was nothing promising in the refrigerator, either, just plain old bread and a container of yogurt. Her plan was ruined before it had even gotten off the ground. Totally discouraged, she had just closed the refrigerator door when she heard a car start up.

Looking out the window, Christina saw that it was Ian's wife's sedan and that Kevin was driving.

Where is he going so early in the morning? Christina wondered, deciding to run out to see. A few minutes later she was on her way to the corner market with Kevin, who had been sent out by his mom for a can of coffee.

"So I'll make her a great breakfast, and then when she's in a good mood, I'll tell her what I want to do," Christina explained as they pulled into the parking lot.

Kevin followed her inside without commenting. He went to the coffee section, while Christina scooped up a basket of strawberries and some fresh bagels.

"Flowers, too?" Kevin asked as Christina tossed a bouquet of lilies onto the checkout counter.

"You bet," Christina replied. "This is important."

"I hate to ruin your grand plan, but I don't think your mom will miraculously change her mind because of a few strawberries and a bagel," Kevin said with a shake of his head as they drove back to White-brook. "She can be pretty stubborn when she wants to be. Just like you."

Christina offered Kevin one of the bagels. "I've been looking for an excuse to do something nice for her anyway. Things have been so busy around White-brook lately. Foaling season was really crazy, and now she's worried about taxes. I know it hasn't helped that I keep pushing her about Star. But if I have to do it one more time, I figure that at least I ought to make it as painless as possible."

After Kevin dropped her off, Christina washed the strawberries and sliced and buttered the bagels. She arranged them on a pretty plate, grabbed the tray and the bud vase, and made her way down to the barn office, hoping her mom hadn't already beaten her there.

"Hang on, Star, I'll be right with you," she called cheerfully when Star's throaty nicker reached her ears.

Christina stepped into the barn office and, seeing that there were no signs of life yet, set the tray on Ashleigh's desk. She arranged the flowers in the bud vase and filled it with water, placing it beside the tray. Then she unrolled the Fair Grounds race schedule and laid it where Ashleigh couldn't miss the bright red circle she had drawn around the Louisiana Derby. Soon she had started the coffeemaker, and the rich aroma of coffee filled the air. As a final touch, she turned on the office heater. Then she made her way to Star's stall.

"Sorry, I had a job to do," Christina explained, sliding the stall door open and clipping his stall guard across the doorway. "If it works, our problems are solved!"

Star nudged her with his nose, and she stroked him while she adjusted his heavy blanket, listening to the familiar morning barn noises that sounded to her like comforting background music. There was the clatter of feed pans as Jonnie started down the aisle. Christina could hear Igor in the stall next to Star, stamping his feet impatiently. Down the aisle, Dazzle whinnied eagerly.

A few minutes later she heard the sound of her mom's boots echo on the barn floor.

Christina turned toward Star's powerful shoulder, inhaling his special scent of horse and hay. "You look first. I can't. Is she smiling or frowning?" she whispered into his warm coat.

Turning, she looked up to see that her mom was giving her an amused look.

"So I step into my office, and I think, *At last! They've finally started room service at Whitebrook.*" Then Ashleigh held up the schedule. "That was before I saw this and realized it was all part of an elaborate plot. Would you by any chance know who was behind it?"

Christina cleared her throat. "I admit it. I made

you breakfast. And you're right. I did kind of have an ulterior motive."

"I suspected it might be you."

Christina rushed on. "So what do you think? Can we enter him in the Louisiana Derby? I mean, if we're going to take him to Fair Grounds anyway . . ."

Her voice trailed off.

"Fine by me," Ashleigh said.

Christina wasn't sure if she believed her ears. "Huh?"

Ashleigh said, "It's a risk, that's for sure. But I stayed up last night and watched Wonder's Kentucky Derby video after you went to bed. I thought about what you said."

Christina hardly dared to breathe as her mom looked away, lost in her thoughts. "Maybe I have been too cautious with Star," Ashleigh finally went on. "The longer you stay in this business, the easier it is to think about everything that can go wrong instead of everything that can go right."

She pulled a piece of straw from the bale standing outside Star's stall and chewed it thoughtfully. "Of course, the more traveled path is from the Florida Derby to the Kentucky Derby, but there have been a few horses who have gone from the Louisiana to the Kentucky."

Christina jumped in. "Black Gold and Grindstone. And there was another Star—Risen Star—a son of Secretariat who won the Preakness and the Belmont after the Louisiana Derby. It's like it's meant to be."

Ashleigh smiled fondly. "It appears you know your Triple Crown history," she laughed. Then a more serious look stole over her face. "There's no doubt that the competition will still be tough, but I think New Orleans will be a better place than Florida to start Star after his hiatus. Since Celtic Mist will be running in the Florida Derby, we won't have to face him until Star gets another race or two under his belt."

"I still think Star could blow Celtic Mist right off the track," Christina said with a flash of anger.

Ashleigh went on as though she hadn't heard Christina. "The only problem is the distance Star will have to travel to get to New Orleans. It's about the same as it is to Florida. It's a long haul."

"But Star traveled all the way to Montana without any problems, and that was just after he got sick. You know he travels well. He always has." Christina spoke quickly, afraid Ashleigh would talk herself out of the whole thing.

Ashleigh shrugged. "Well, I thought about that, too. Anyway, it's too late now—I've already made the call."

Christina swallowed expectantly.

"He's entered. We're on!" Ashleigh told her.

Christina leaped to hug her mom over the stall guard, still not quite believing it was true.

"Thanks," she murmured against Ashleigh's scratchy wool jacket, feeling hot tears of relief press against her eyelids.

"We're cutting it close, though. The Louisiana Derby is only a few days away," Ashleigh added when Christina had broken away. "I think we should give him the day off today, but we'll breeze him again tomorrow. And then we'd better get him down there."

"Okay," Christina said. She felt so happy, she would have agreed to anything her mother said.

"Oh, and Chris," Ashleigh said, "next time you need to change my mind about something, remember that I like onion bagels better than plain."

Christina nodded and flung her arms around Star, wanting to laugh and cry at the same time.

"Did you hear that, Star?" she murmured to him. "We've got a race to win."

"So I'm off to New Orleans," Christina explained to her school friends at lunch that day.

"Cool," said Katie. "I went there once during Mardi Gras. It was kind of wild, but the city is really pretty. New Orleans has these old parts that are kind of spooky, with Spanish moss dripping everywhere and these neat old buildings."

"I'm not going sightseeing, so I doubt I'll bump into any ghosts or anything," Christina said, laughing. "I'm going down there for one reason, and that's to race."

"Well, maybe your racetrack will be haunted," Katie added hopefully. "Anyway, that's great news. I'll definitely watch your race on TV."

Just before the bell rang, Christina went to the pay phone and tried to call Parker. She knew he'd be in classes, so she left the good news on his answering machine.

Christina floated through school the rest of the day. That evening she pounced on the phone when Melanie called to fill everyone in on the horses and racing results at Gulfstream.

"Guess what, Mel?" Christina practically shouted into the phone, cutting her cousin off in midsentence.

"I can't guess. Tell me," Melanie replied.

"No, you have to guess."

"Okay, you've decided to give up racing and you're going back to eventing?"

Christina glared at the phone. Sometimes Melanie could be so annoying. "Very funny. No, it's better than that. My mom's letting me enter Star in the Louisiana Derby!"

"The Louisiana Derby? Wow. Cool. Well, better than cool, I guess."

"You *guess?* Did you know that a bunch of horses

that won the Louisiana Derby went on to win the Triple Crown? It's way, way, way better than cool."

"Yeah, well, *great!*" Melanie shouted so loudly that Christina pulled the receiver from her ear for a second.

Christina rushed on. "My mom wasn't thrilled with the idea, but she decided it might be a way to get Star in a prep race without facing Celtic Mist yet. So you and Image will just have to blow Brad's overrated horse away yourselves for now."

"What do you mean?" Melanie asked.

"What do you mean, 'What do you mean?'" Christina was really annoyed now. She wasn't in the mood for any more joking around. This was all too serious. "Just what I said."

"But Celtic Mist isn't here," Melanie said quietly. "Some of the other Townsend horses are here. The word around the backside is that Celtic Mist is headed to New Orleans. For the Louisiana Derby."

Christina groaned as she set down the phone. Sure, she'd been confident when she'd told her mom Star was ready to take on Celtic Mist. But all of a sudden she wasn't so sure. Maybe some of her mom's hesitation was rubbing off on her.

Well, there was no backing out now.

Parker confirmed what Melanie had said when Christina spoke to him soon afterward. "But don't you worry about it," he said in his usual confident way. "The best horse will win."

Christina didn't reply to that. Even though she knew her boyfriend and his dad didn't see eye to eye, she didn't want to make him say straight out which horse he thought was best. Instead, she steered the subject back to his training.

After she hung up, Christina couldn't help wondering if Parker was still harboring a grudge because she hadn't told him of her plans to put off college. Maybe she ought to call him back and try to talk to him about it once more.

Don't be such a worrywart, she told herself as she set the phone back in the cradle. She had enough on her mind with Star's race—the race that would help decide if the big colt was ready to be considered a serious Triple Crown contender or simply another one of the many horses destined to be forgotten by racing fans as the big day drew closer.

She wandered into the family room, where Ashleigh was sorting through some papers.

"What's up, Chris?" her mom asked, looking up from her work.

Christina plopped onto the sofa. "Celtic Mist is going to race in the Louisiana Derby," she said with a groan.

Ashleigh studied her face. "You look worried. I thought you were so convinced that Star could beat Celtic Mist easily."

"I *was.* I mean, I *am,*" Christina began. "But like

you said, maybe it would have been better if Star had had a little more time before running against him."

"So I guess this means Star will have his work cut out for him," Ashleigh said evenly.

"Yeah," Christina muttered. "He sure will."

"No need to be discouraged," Ashleigh said. "So maybe it isn't the way we would have planned it, but we have to face whatever challenge comes. The only thing we can do is get Star in the best shape we can so that he'll be ready on race day."

By the time Tuesday rolled around and her dad had flown back from Florida, Christina's head was in a whirl from all the preparation. There was so much to do in such a short time. Ashleigh had decided that Naomi, Dani, and Joe would go down in the van with Star. To cut down on missed days at school, Christina would fly to New Orleans just before race day.

Christina checked and cleaned the equipment that would be going with Star. Assembling feed, feed buckets, tack, and veterinary supplies took hours.

"I'll never get everything done," she wailed to her mom that evening while she set the table for dinner. "Tomorrow after school I need to roll a hundred bandages, bleach towels, and clean a huge pile of tack."

"I hate to add to your woes, but tomorrow after school we're going into Lexington to get you some new clothes."

"For what? I don't have time," Christina said quickly.

"You need to make time," Ashleigh said. "Look, neither of us likes shopping, but you're going to be even busier these next few months, and believe me, you'll have even less time."

"But I don't need anything," Christina protested, tucking one shoe behind the other so her mom wouldn't see that the sole had come unglued.

But her mom was too quick for her. Ashleigh's eyes slid to her shoes. "I'd rest my case right there, except I feel compelled to add that your jeans are so worn, they're threadbare. And your shirts and sweaters are practically coming apart in the wash. You take good care of your horses, but it wouldn't hurt to pay a little attention to yourself sometimes."

Christina looked down at the khaki pants and T-shirt she was wearing. "My clothes are just fine. I'm not entering a fashion show or a beauty pageant."

Her dad strode into the room just then. "No, but you're pretty enough that you should," he said, picking up his address book.

"Oh, Dad," Christina said, and rolled her eyes.

"It's not about fashion shows," Ashleigh said quietly. "But you are representing Whitebrook, and every time Star wins from now on, he'll be drawing a great deal of attention to the farm. Like it or not, you'll both be in the spotlight. You're a professional now—don't forget it."

"So I should get all dolled up like Lavinia Town-send?" Christina said with a scowl.

Christina saw her dad crack a grin, but Ashleigh shook her head at him. "I don't think you have to go that far," he said. "Listen to your mom. She's done this a time or two," Mike added, winking at Christina as he walked out.

Ashleigh went on. "I'm talking a couple of pairs of jeans, a sweater or two. Nice shirts. Some shoes and maybe a suit. Never forget that this is a business."

"Fine." Christina was too tired to put up a fight. And anyway, in her heart of hearts she knew her mom was right. It was easy to get so involved in the day-to-day of barn activities that she could completely forget there was a world out there where performance mattered, but appearances said something as well.

Christina had been standing with a group of her friends by the flagpole when she saw her mom's car pulling into the parking lot after school that after-noon.

"Imagine having your mom have to *command* you to shop," Lindsey said wonderingly. The pretty blond soccer player was a serious jock, but she usually turned up at school wearing trendy outfits. "My mom is always complaining that I buy too many clothes."

"But you do," one of her friends assured her good-naturedly. "Don't forget I had to go with you to return those three skirts you bought the other day because you already had six others like them."

"Stop exaggerating!" Lindsey grinned and shrugged. She turned to Christina. "Want me to go with you? I could be your personal shopper," she joked.

Katie frowned and wagged a playful finger at Lindsey. "I don't think Christina would fit in at the track wearing the kind of clothes you like."

Lindsey shrugged. "Yeah, probably not."

"There's the Mall Express. Well, see you guys," Christina said as Ashleigh's car pulled up in front of the school steps.

Christina wished she could just go home to White-brook instead. There was so much work to be done at the barn, and she didn't see how her mom could stand to be away for the afternoon.

"Don't look so glum," Ashleigh said as Christina slid into the front seat. "We'll speed-shop, and afterward I'll buy you a smoothie at Bernard's."

Christina shrugged. "How about a trip to the tack shop, too?"

Ashleigh smiled. "You got it," she said.

On the drive to the mall, Christina and her mom talked about Star and their racing strategy. By the time they arrived at the mall, Christina was so excited about the race that even the prospect of trying on clothes didn't bring her down.

Two hours later she and her mom were finished.

They rounded off the trip by wandering around Christina's favorite tack shop. Afterward they collapsed into the booth at Bernard's, where they ordered their favorite strawberry-and-banana concoctions.

"I'd say that that was pretty successful," Ashleigh said, eyeing the bags they had crammed into the booth with them.

"Two pairs of jeans, two sweaters, one pair of shoes—and a navy blue suit." Christina ticked off the list. "Now I won't have to shop for at least a year!"

"Unless you grow," her mom said.

"I'd better not!" Christina said hotly. "I'm already pretty tall for a jockey."

"Well, at least Star won't be embarrassed anymore because he has a jockey with holes in her shoes," Ashleigh joked.

"Speaking of which," Christina said, anxiously looking at her watch, "can we go home now?"

Ashleigh smiled and stood up. "By all means," she said. "We've got a race to run!"

8

"SEE YOU IN A COUPLE OF DAYS," CHRISTINA SAID, AFFEC-tionately pulling Star's ears. "You be a good boy and do what Dani tells you, okay?"

She had just finished loading Star into the van while her dad talked with the driver, a cheerful, stocky woman whom Christina's mom and dad had been friends with for years. The words "Longview Farm" were spelled out in bold green lettering on the side of the van.

"Everything's here," Kevin shouted from the van's tack room, where he had loaded everything that Star, Dazzle, and Rhapsody would need for the next few days. He opened the door and hopped out of the van.

Christina bent down and adjusted Star's thick

shipping wraps for the umpteenth time. She examined the cushiony rubber flooring and the padding on the walls that would provide protection against bumps. Satisfied that things were in order, Christina rechecked the hay net and smoothed Star's blanket across his back. Patting his sleek neck one last time, she walked down the rubber-covered ramp.

Dani and Joe tossed their duffel bags in the storage area of the van.

"This is so exciting," Christina heard Dani say to Joe. "I've never been to New Orleans before."

"You're going to love it," Joe drawled. "The food's so good, you're going to put on a few pounds."

Dani glared at him. "You're funny, Kisner. In case you've forgotten, I'm not going there to eat. I'll have too much work to do. And so will you."

Christina listened to their good-natured banter enviously, wishing she were going down to Fair Grounds early as well. She let out a long sigh and helped pull out the wooden blocks that had been wedged under the van tires to prevent the van from rolling while the horses were being loaded.

When the ramp was up and the last latch secured, Mike went over to thank his friend for giving the Whitebrook horses a lift. Dani and Joe climbed into the cab. Dani rolled down her window.

"Don't worry, Chris. I'll take good care of Star till you get to New Orleans," she called over the roar of the engine. "I won't let anything happen to him, I promise."

"I know you won't," Christina assured the groom. She knew that Dani still felt bad that Star had gotten sick at the Belmont track all those months ago while under her care. It hadn't been Dani's fault or anyone else's. It was just a horrible case of back luck.

Still, as Christina watched the van pull down Whitebrook's long drive, she couldn't help feeling uneasy at being separated from Star.

Mike and Kevin stood by her on the drive. "He'll be fine," Mike said, as if reading her mind. "Naomi will fly down there tomorrow and get everyone used to the track, and you'll be there before you know it." He leaned over and ruffled Christina's hair. "Take these wheelbarrows back to the barn while I go make a couple of calls, will you?"

Christina grabbed one of the empty wheelbarrows they had used to wheel bags of feed and supplements over to the van and followed Kevin back to the feed room.

"Kind of exciting, huh?" Kevin asked after they had dropped off the wheelbarrows.

Christina nodded. "Yeah. It's weird, too. For the first time, racing Star in the Kentucky Derby is not just some distant wish. It feels like it could actually become real."

They made they way over to the boards to see which horses they were signed up to exercise that morning. With three horses headed for Louisiana and another three in Florida, there weren't many left to work.

Kevin's gaze followed Christina's to the blank space next to Star's name. Grabbing a marker, Kevin wrote in, "Gone to Louisiana Derby!"

"There," he said triumphantly. "That looks better than a big blank space. Now it's official."

Under the "Barn Notes" section of the board, he added, "Dear trainers: Please excuse Star from workouts for the next few days. He's off pursuing greatness in New Orleans." Then he set down the marker with a flourish.

Christina smiled. "You goof," she said, playfully cuffing Kevin. But then she traced the word *Derby* next to Star's name with her finger, saying, "Star's first big step toward the Triple Crown. After the Louisiana Derby, who knows? The Blue Grass Stakes? Then Kentucky Derby, here we come!"

Kevin whistled a few bars of "My Old Kentucky Home" for good measure. Then his eyes grew serious. "It's great that everything is going your way," he said a little wistfully.

"Finally," Christina said, turning to look at her friend. She knew that he was thinking about his own dreams. "You haven't heard anything about your soccer scholarships, have you?"

Kevin shook his head. "One of my teammates got

picked up at Kentucky State. He got a full scholarship—tuition, books, the works. He really likes the soccer coach and the program there. I'm happy for him, I just hope the recruiters won't overlook me."

"Oh, Kevin, it'll all work out," Christina said, trying to cheer him up.

Kevin looked down ruefully at his knee. "I don't know. People tend not to want to take chances on you when you've been out for half the season with an injury."

Christina whacked him playfully on the shoulder. "Don't be negative. You've been such a solid player. Your name is legend at Henry Clay. I just know some school will make you a huge offer. Don't worry, Kevin, your dreams are going to come true, too."

Kevin pushed a lock of red hair off his forehead. "Well, if they don't, I guess I can always work here as an exercise rider or something."

"You say that as if it were a bad thing," Christina said, laughing.

"No, it's not bad," Kevin replied. "It's just that I want to do other things, as well."

"I know," Christina said, understanding completely.

Kevin shrugged. "It's easier for you and Melanie," he said. "The two of you know what you want, and all of it is right here at Whitebrook. For me, the future isn't such a sure thing."

"You think our future is a sure thing?" Christina

said, shocked. "Come on, Kevin. You've been around long enough to know that anything can happen in horse racing. Horse farms can go bust, horses can get sick, or jockeys can get hurt—and those are just some of the things that can go wrong. I don't think you can find a more uncertain future than racing."

Kevin blew out a big breath of air and turned toward the tack room. "Let's not talk about it anymore, okay? I think we're making ourselves crazy talking about the future like this. Who knows what's going to happen?"

Christina chewed on her lip thoughtfully as she grabbed her helmet and started toward the track, where Cindy was waiting with a horse ready to be exercised. She had been having more and more talks like this with her friends lately, talks about the future that made her realize that their childhoods were ending. It was scary and exciting all at the same time.

Christina fastened her chin strap and approached Cindy, hoping she wouldn't be in a crabby mood.

But Cindy was smiling sympathetically. "Bet you wish you were in that van right now with Star, huh?" Cindy was holding one of Terminator's fillies. The young horse was prancing in place, raring to go.

Christina nodded. "Yeah. I definitely do. Unfortunately, I have to go to school. I'm flying down with Mom in a couple of days."

As she gave Christina a leg up onto the filly's back,

Cindy sighed. "I'd give anything to be racing again, at any track."

Christina picked up the reins, not sure what to say. "You'll be back riding before you know it," Christina said, risking one of Cindy's withering glances. If there was anything Cindy hated, it was sympathy.

Cindy's eyes had an unreadable expression. "That's not what the doctor said. Anyway, I'm glad to see that Star's in racing shape again. He looks great to me, and his times have been fantastic."

Christina brightened at Cindy's words. After all, Cindy had raced everywhere and had seen a lot of horseflesh. She tended to know what she was talking about when it came to horses. If she thought Star was ready, that counted for something.

"Still, you never can tell," Cindy said, releasing the filly's head. "He hasn't raced in a while, so don't expect too much."

Don't listen to her, Christina told herself savagely as she urged the Terminator filly out onto the track. *She doesn't know Star like I do. I know he's ready. I've never been more sure of anything in my life.*

School that day seemed to take longer than ever. Christina had always liked school, but lately it was all she could do to keep her mind on what her teachers were saying. The subjects she was studying seemed to be so unrelated to the rest of her life. Take calculus, for example. How could knowing calculus help her ride better? She smiled, remembering how many times she had teased Melanie when Melanie had brought up the same argument against school. Now she was beginning to understand what Melanie meant.

Drumming her fingers against her desk, she pictured Melanie riding the sometimes unruly Image at Gulfstream. Then her mind switched to Star, somewhere on a highway on his way to Fair Grounds. Had she remembered to check his water bucket? she thought worriedly.

"Miss Reese, would you mind joining our discussion of Steinbeck?" The voice of her English teacher penetrated her thoughts.

Christina flushed and tried unsuccessfully to transport her brain from Star's van back to room 122 at Henry Clay High School.

As the day dragged on, Christina found herself becoming even more distracted. Her friends kept giving each other strange looks whenever she walked up to them. Christina was sure they noticed how out of sorts she was. *Oh, well,* she thought. *There isn't anything I can do about it.* She couldn't pay attention to anything, not when she was wondering how Star was traveling and if he would be comfortable at the strange track.

After school Christina headed down to the barn, glumly walking past Star's empty stall. She and Kevin did their barn chores together quickly and silently.

Since there wasn't that much to do, Kevin took off early, leaving Christina to blanket the horses and test the automatic waterers in the training barn. Ashleigh went up to the house to start dinner while Christina made a final check to see that everything was secure and locked down for the night. Finally she finished up and headed toward the house.

That's weird, Christina thought, glancing at the kitchen window. *Why's the house so dark? Mom went up to start dinner an hour ago.*

As Christina stepped into the kitchen and groped for the switch, the lights flashed on, momentarily blinding her.

"Surprise!"

Christina stepped back, startled at the shouting. As her eyes adjusted to the light, she saw the faces of her friends, who were crowded around a decorated kitchen table piled high with food and sodas.

"What?" Christina sputtered. "What are you guys doing here?"

She scanned the room quickly. Katie, Parker, Kevin, and Lindsey were there, throwing up handfuls of metallic blue confetti. Her parents were standing with Sam Nelson and her husband, Tor, by the stove. Ian, Beth, and Cindy came in from the hallway. Christina guessed that they had sneaked in the front door.

Katie ran over and hugged her. "It's a Good Luck

Star surprise party!" she shouted, pointing to a large banner hanging on the wall. "Go Star Go!" it read in blue-and-white checkered letters—Whitebrook Farm's colors.

"You guys did all this for me and Star?" Christina asked, taking in the balloons and the cake decorated with red roses and a gold racing trophy.

"We sure did," Parker confessed, presenting her with an orchid. "Here is the first of many more orchids we're sure you and Star will be receiving in New Orleans."

Christina's face flushed happily. She knew from her reading that the orchid was the official flower of the Fair Grounds Race Course. Maybe it was a peace offering from Parker, a way of saying he was sorry he had given her a hard time about her college plans.

Kevin and Lindsey stepped forward, grabbing Christina's arms excitedly. "So, were you surprised?" Lindsey asked.

"Definitely!" Christina said, laughing. "It was so dark in here, I thought Mom had forgotten my dinner."

"I nearly blew it at school today," Katie added. "I almost asked you whether or not you still liked carrot cake. I hope you do, because that's what my mom baked."

"Yum," Christina said hungrily.

But hungry as she was, Christina could manage to eat only a small slice of cake. She hoped she didn't hurt Katie's feelings, but her stomach was too filled with butterflies.

After everyone had loaded their plates, they went into the family room, which was also decorated. Gold horseshoes and Derby posters festooned with streamers were pasted to the walls. Christina and Parker sat on the floor in front of the fireplace, while their other friends squished onto the sofa, balancing their plates on their knees.

They chattered happily about horses and races, and after a while Christina's butterflies drifted away, replaced with a kind of calm contentment. This was one of those moments in life that she'd never forget, she realized. Here she was, surrounded by some of the people who mattered the most to her and looking forward to an exciting race. She thought about Melanie and wished her cousin could be there, too. Toasting her silently with her plastic cup filled with soda, she took a sip and leaned cozily against Parker.

She was surprised when he stood up quickly, and she almost spilled her soda. But she didn't have time to consider his strange move, because just then the doorbell chimed.

Immediately Ashleigh jumped up to answer it, but Katie stopped her. "Do you mind if I answer it?" Christina's mom looked puzzled, but she nodded.

Seconds later Katie led a strange woman into the family room. The new arrival was wearing silky, flowing robes and carrying a brightly colored tapestry bag.

"This is Madame X," she said in a breathless voice. "She's come to read the future."

Christina grinned and shook her head as Madame X made a dramatic entrance. Trust Katie to hire a fortune-teller to come to the party.

Madame X took out a velvety purple cloth, which she draped over the coffee table. On it she placed a crystal ball, and then she invited the guests to come have their fortunes told.

Christina watched for a moment as Madame X searched the crystal ball for Lindsey's future. Then she noticed that Parker had disappeared, so she got up and went into the kitchen, where she found him slicing another piece of cake.

"Hi," she said. "Aren't you going to go have your fortune told?" she asked playfully.

Parker shrugged. "I don't believe in that stuff," he said.

Christina frowned. She didn't believe in fortune-telling, either, but it was strange that the normally fun-loving Parker wouldn't be willing to play along.

"I guess you're still mad at me because I didn't talk to you first about not going to college next year," she said. "Do you want to talk about it now?"

Parker set down his cake plate and turned toward her. "No, I'm not mad. Whatever makes you happy is fine with me."

Christina looked into Parker's smoky gray eyes. "Do you mean that?" she asked.

Parker looked away and nodded. "Sorry. I know I've been acting kind of strange lately. I think I'm just stressed about the Olympic trials and all. I didn't mean to make you worry. Come on, let's go back and join the party."

Christina wasn't entirely convinced, but she followed Parker back into the family room and resumed her spot by the fireplace. From there she watched her friends crowd around the table and listened to their laughter and chatter.

Suddenly Madame X's reedy voice cut through the noise. "I see something," she said solemnly. She peered closer at her crystal ball. "Christina Reese, would you please make yourself known and come here?"

Parker nudged her, and Christina stood up and walked over to the table.

The fortune-teller picked up the crystal ball and turned it, as if to see better from another angle. Christina bit her lip to keep from laughing out loud.

"I see a star in your future," Madame X said loudly.

"Considering that's her horse's name, that's no biggie," Kevin blurted from across the room. The fortune-teller gave him a fierce look.

Christina bit her lip even harder and tried to look serious.

The woman frowned and peered more closely at the ball. "Ah, there's more."

Feeling slightly foolish, Christina found herself leaning in to see if she could see what the woman was talking about. The ball looked completely clear to her.

"You don't have the sight," the fortune-teller said, pulling the crystal ball away from Christina.

"No, I guess not," Christina said.

The fortune-teller put her finger to her lips. "Shush. I'll do the talking. Hmmm. What's this? I see a heart that's tested."

"Whooo, watch it, Parker," someone teased.

Christina glanced at Parker, who grinned and shook his head. "Don't look at me," he yelped.

Suddenly the woman grabbed Christina's hand, her blood-red nails contrasting with Christina's short, unpolished ones. "I see a race," Madame X said, her voice rising in a way that made Christina shiver. "I see a fast horse. He's—he's—"

"He's what?" Christina couldn't help herself. She really wanted to know.

The woman released her hold on Christina's hand. "He's running."

"Well, duh. That's what he does!" Kevin cut in.

The fortune-teller shot him another look before staring into her crystal ball once more.

The room was silent, and Christina could feel her heart beat.

This is so silly, she thought. *I can't believe I'm getting worked up about this.*

"I see a surprise."

Christina waited to hear more, but the woman merely ran her hand over the crystal ball and shook her head.

"What kind of surprise?" Christina asked, her voice quavering

"A good one or a bad one?" Katie called out.

Madame X shrugged. "That's it. That's all I know."

"That's it?" Christina asked, not sure if she was more annoyed with Madame X or with herself for wanting to know. "Well, thank you . . . I guess."

Christina returned to her seat and whispered to Parker, "What do you think that meant?"

"I think it meant she just remembered she had another party to go to and she had to get out of here in a hurry," Parker joked.

Christina rolled her eyes, but when she saw how quickly the fortune-teller packed up and left, she decided Parker might be right.

Still, she couldn't help wondering what kind of surprise Madame X had meant.

At least she didn't predict disaster, Christina told herself.

9

"WOW, IS IT ALWAYS THIS WARM DOWN HERE?" CHRISTINA asked, stepping out of the terminal at New Orleans International Airport, where the languid heat and humidity enveloped her immediately. Joe was waiting for her at the curb.

"Yup," said Joe cheerfully. "You get used to it."

Already sweating as she and Joe hoisted her suitcases into the trunk, Christina peeled off her blue fleece jacket and threw it in on top of her luggage.

"I don't think I'll be needing that anymore," she said.

"Probably not," Joe agreed, slamming the trunk lid closed.

"Hey, buddy, move that car," groused a traffic officer. "This is a red zone."

"We're going, we're going," the groom muttered.

"Thanks for picking me up, Joe," Christina said breathlessly as she jumped into the passenger seat. "Whose car is this, anyway?"

The groom pulled away from the curb and entered the steady stream of traffic heading toward the main road. "Oh, it belongs to one of my track friends," he said. "The thing's held together with chewing gum and baling wire. I hope it can get us back to Fair Grounds. Otherwise we have a long walk ahead of us."

Christina smiled and tried to ignore the strange sounds the engine was making. The last thing she wanted was to be delayed by a breakdown. For one thing, she didn't think she would last very long in the warm, humid air, which threatened to suffocate her. Plus she couldn't wait to see Star again. No matter how often she was separated from Star, she never got used to it.

Immediately Christina began pelting Joe with questions about how Star and the other horses were settling in. Joe answered patiently, pretending not to know she had called to check on Star every night since they had arrived.

"Star settled himself right in," Joe said. "I think he likes it here in New Orleans. It's a little warmer and wetter than he's used to, but with the stall door open, it's not unbearable. The good news is we get some good cross breezes in our row."

Satisfied that Star was all right, Christina looked out the window, taking in the scenery, which was so different from that of Kentucky. The trees seemed closer together in New Orleans, and they were draped with Spanish moss. The houses they passed were painted with bright colors, and many of them were surrounded by ornate iron fences. Christina shivered as they passed an old graveyard, filled with elaborate monuments that looked as though they were hundreds of years old.

"Wow, this place is kind of creepy," she exclaimed.

Joe chuckled. "Yeah, but it's an easygoing town, too. People are really laid back down here. They don't take things too seriously."

Christina pushed back a lock of sweaty hair. She, for one, would be taking things seriously while she was here. The Louisiana Derby was too important to her and Star not to take seriously.

"So where's your mom? I thought she was coming, too," Joe said as they turned onto the highway.

Christina nodded. "She was supposed to, but this morning, just before we were to leave for the airport, Perfect Heart foaled. A filly. She seems really weak, and Mom was worried, so she wanted to stay behind. She's going to try to catch another flight tonight or tomorrow."

Joe nodded but didn't speak for a while. Traffic was heavy, and he frowned as he maneuvered the temperamental car between lanes.

"Uh, Chris, I guess I might as well tell you now,"

Joe said when they neared Fair Grounds. "You'll never guess who's stabled right next door to us."

Christina groaned. "Let me guess. Celtic Mist. I knew he was coming here, but is he really right next door?"

"You got it. I didn't want to tell you earlier because I figured I could talk management into moving us. Then when I found out we had to stay put, I didn't want to get you upset before you got here."

"Great. That's all we need," Christina muttered.

"Tell me about it. Brad and Lavinia have been hanging around like flies. Yesterday they walked past with some hoity-toity friends talking in loud voices about how amazing it was that 'poor old Star' survived the trip down here. They can't believe he's fit enough to be seen at the track."

"Oh, why couldn't they have sent Celtic Mist to Florida?" Christina grumbled.

"That's not all," Joe said, chuckling to himself. "Dani had a little accident right about then. She happened to trip with a bucket of dirty water and 'accidentally' soaked Brad's suit and Lavinia's designer shoes."

Christina laughed as she pictured the scene. "Good old Dani."

Joe nodded. "They weren't too pleased, but it shut them up."

"So what are people saying about Celtic Mist?" Christina asked casually.

"That he's the one to beat," Joe answered. "But

Naomi has been watching the works, and she says she thinks Star has a real chance to beat him. It'll be a close one, but I'd put my two bucks on Star any day."

"Thanks," Christina said gratefully.

They pulled into the Fair Grounds stabling area, and she gazed about her at the towering red-roofed grandstands in the distance. Compared to Keeneland or Churchill Downs, it looked modern and very big.

"Don't look so worried," Joe said. "The facilities are great here."

Christina twisted a lock of her hair nervously. "I'm not worried about the facilities."

"Well, don't worry about Star, either. The fans still remember him—they adore him."

"Yeah, but the handicappers know he hasn't raced for a long time," Christina replied.

"And they won't believe how fast he can run," Joe replied, flashing his badge at the gate guard.

By the time she climbed out of the car, Christina felt herself slipping into worry mode. She knew she was being ridiculous. After all, Star had turned in some of his best times ever before he left for Louisiana.

Nothing has changed since then, she told herself firmly.

She took her luggage out of the trunk and tied her fleece jacket around her waist. Glancing around the stable area, Christina could see that it was teeming with people and horses. Joe pointed the way to the Whitebrook stalls and took off to return the car keys to the car's owner.

Christina waved hello to a few trainers and exercise riders she knew, trying to lose herself in the excitement of the track. Jazz music was pouring from the sound system, setting a jaunty mood. She'd never been to Fair Grounds before, and it was fun to take everything in. She knew it was steeped in history, originating in the 1800s, but the grandstands had been rebuilt after burning down a few years ago. The new facility was sleek and functional but charming at the same time. The stalls she passed on the way to the Whitebrook stalls were large and airy. It was even nicer than she had anticipated.

Several people were gathered around a stall just up ahead, and Christina felt herself stiffen when she saw Brad and Lavinia in the crowd.

That must be Celtic Mist's stall, she thought.

"Isn't he the most gorgeous animal you've ever seen?" Christina heard Lavinia squeal.

"He sure is," someone else said.

"He should be," came Brad's arrogant voice. "His breeding's impeccable. Plus he's got conformation and speed. It doesn't get any better than this."

Oh, please! Christina thought, wanting to gag.

Turning her head, she tried to make herself invisible as she walked past. She didn't want Brad or Lavinia to see her. She wasn't in the mood for the snide remarks she knew they would send her way. Luckily, the Townsends paid no attention when she walked by.

"Too busy bragging," Christina muttered under her breath.

Star's whinny pierced the air as Christina approached, and she ran the last few feet, calling his name. Happily she swung open the door to Star's roomy stall and threw her arms around his copper-colored neck.

"Did you miss me, boy?" she asked the colt, who busied himself searching her thoroughly for carrots. He was rewarded when he found the carrot stash she had stuffed into her shoulder bag.

Dani emerged from Dazzle's stall, pitchfork in hand. "Hi," she said, her voice nearly drowned out by the catchy music pumping out of invisible speakers throughout the backside. Dani dropped a load of dirty straw into the wheelbarrow outside Dazzle's stall and wiped away the sweat that was beading on her brow.

Christina patted Dazzle, then walked over to Rhapsody's empty stall.

"Where's Rhapsody?" she asked.

"Naomi's got him out on the track," Dani called over as she pushed the wheelbarrow full of dirty straw past Christina on the way to the manure pile. "You're going to love New Orleans. We're right near the French Quarter. We got breakfast there, and I saved you a beignet—it's like a fried doughnut. I'm already addicted. There's also a cup of chicory coffee. It's probably cold, but it will still taste good."

"Thanks," Christina said, suddenly realizing how hungry she was.

Just before Dani turned the corner she called out, "The food's in the feed room, just inside the door."

Christina wandered into the feed room and spotted a paper sack sitting on top of a burlap feed bag. Pulling out the beignet, she took a big bite.

"Yum," she said out loud, wolfing down the rest of it. "I can see why she's addicted."

Wiping her sugary fingers on her jeans, she took a sip of the cold coffee. She nearly choked when she tasted the oddly flavored liquid.

"Nasty!" she exclaimed, tossing the cup into the nearest trash barrel. The thick, heavy brew didn't do anything for her stomach, which was already churning from nerves.

Settle down, Christina commanded her stomach. *There's no reason to be so nervous.*

Grabbing a grooming box, Christina set to work brushing Star's coppery coat until it gleamed. When she was finished, she stood back and watched the light bounce off his burnished shoulder.

"Talk about gorgeous," she murmured before grabbing a hoof pick.

Christina had just finished picking out Star's

hooves when she heard footsteps right outside Star's stall. The footsteps stopped, and Christina winced as Lavinia's brittle laughter floated through the air. Feeling the hairs rise on her neck, she turned around to face the Townsends. She was going to have to deal with them sooner or later. She might as well get it over with.

"Hello," she said.

"Oh, hello," Lavinia replied, giving her a cool glance. Though it was still morning, Lavinia was already dressed to the nines in a beige linen suit and lots of gold jewelry. To Christina, she looked totally out of place among the casually dressed grooms, jockeys, and trainers scattered around the backside.

Brad peered into the stall. "Now that you're here, maybe you can keep your help in order. That little groom of yours made a real mess yesterday."

Serves you right, Christina thought fiercely, remembering what Joe had told her about the "bath" that Dani had given the Townsends the day before. She wished she had been there to witness their humiliation.

"We were shocked to find out your mother had decided to enter Star in the Louisiana Derby," Brad drawled, his eyes sliding condescendingly over Star. "You do realize this is a serious prep race, don't you?"

"Yes, I do," Christina said. She opened the stall door, causing Brad to back up and step into a pile of soiled straw that had fallen off a passing wheelbarrow.

"I was just as surprised to hear that you entered Celtic Mist. I thought you would have kept him in Florida."

Brad wiped his shoe on the cement, his eyes never leaving Christina. "Well, he was doing very well, of course, but he's already proven himself there. We thought we'd see how the competition was here in Louisiana."

He looked disdainfully at Star and added, "Of course, if Star's any indication of the level of competition here, I don't know. It doesn't look like much, does it?"

Christina smiled icily, hiding her hot thoughts as best she could. "May the best horse win."

Lavinia toyed with a glittery bracelet. "Oh, he will," she said sweetly. "Perhaps you hadn't heard that Celtic Mist set a track record during his work just now. Everyone is talking about it."

To anyone else, Christina would have offered her congratulations, but she couldn't possibly add to the Townsends' inflated egos.

Lavinia wrinkled her nose in a frown. "What was his time again?" she said, as if she'd forgotten. "Oh, yes. Now I remember." Then she rattled off a time that was two seconds faster than Star's latest workout time. Christina felt her face grow pale.

"Oh, dear. I didn't mean to make you worry," Lavinia added, putting her hand to her mouth in an elaborately insincere gesture. "But your Star had his day, and now it's Mist's turn."

Oh, go away! Christina thought, smoldering. She

wished her mother were there with her. Ashleigh always had a sharp retort for Brad. For the millionth time Christina wondered how people like Brad and Lavinia had ever had a son as nice as Parker.

She glared at the Townsends as they walked away. Then she kicked viciously at a clump of bedding.

"Let me guess. The Townsends clued you in about Celtic Mist's workout," Naomi said, leading Rhapsody into her stall. Rhapsody had just had a bath and was covered with a light fly sheet.

Christina sighed. "How did you know?"

"Your face told it all. They sure know how to rub it in," Naomi said.

"I would have found out anyway," Christina said resignedly. "Well, good for Celtic Mist. I guess we've got our work cut out for us."

Naomi nodded. "Maybe. There's no doubt that Celtic Mist is fast. But Star's got way more heart," she said emphatically. "I've been leading him around the last couple of days, so he's used to everything. It's time to get him out on the track. Are you ready?"

No, Christina thought, but she nodded, trying to appear confident. It wasn't going to be easy taking Star out on the same track where Celtic Mist had just set a record.

"Let me go change and get my stuff," Christina said with a brightness she didn't feel. "Star and I will meet you by the gap."

124

"See you there," Naomi replied.

A few minutes later Christina reached the gap and looked out onto the track. Since it was fairly late in the morning, most of the works were already finished. A few horses were out, but they seemed to be galloping in slow motion in the hot, moist air. As a black horse passed by the rail in front of Star, the chestnut colt stamped impatiently.

Naomi let go of the reins, and Christina urged Star forward, taking a deep breath as he stepped onto the soft footing.

Christina felt a shiver of anticipation travel down her spine. In just two days she would be right here, shooting out the starting gate. She gazed around her at the vast grandstands looming in the distance and tried to imagine how they would look on the day of the Louisiana Derby, crammed with spectators. Squeezing Star into a jog, Christina tried to force her thoughts back to their workout.

"Outta my way," snarled a voice from behind her.

Christina veered to the right, even though she knew she had left plenty of room at the rail for the faster horses. A jockey on a gray horse whipped past her. Watching the horse and rider as they pounded ahead, Christina felt sure she had seen the rider before.

She had just taken Star into an easy gallop when it hit her. It was George Valdez, the jockey who had bullied her mercilessly when she had first begun to race

Star. He'd started out by making cracks in the jockeys' lounge. Then he had teamed up with another low-life jockey to box Star in during a race so that she wound up finishing way behind. Another time he'd managed to get Christina temporarily suspended from racing through no fault of her own.

I can't believe he's here, Christina thought. *With my luck, he'll be riding Celtic Mist in the Derby.*

Sure enough, when Christina checked the program after she'd finished their workout and given Star a bath, she saw George's name next to Celtic Mist's. She dropped the program onto a lawn chair Dani had set up outside the feed room and sighed.

Nothing has gone right since I got here.

She tried to convince herself that it made no difference. After all, though she and George had been at odds, they had finally forged a sort of shaky truce. Christina had stood up to him, and since then there hadn't been any problems.

Still, Christina couldn't shake the bad feeling she had had ever since she arrived at Fair Grounds. She had heard that New Orleans was a city filled with ancient superstitions. Had she come here only to find that Star's luck was taking a turn for the worse?

After Star was put away, Christina cleaned tack and tried to lose herself in the jazz music blasting from the speakers. After a while she couldn't help noticing the crowds of spectators that had begun converging on the stable area.

Some would stop at Star's stall momentarily, a few people recognizing the horse from his earlier races. But most of them hurried on past and gathered around Celtic Mist's stall. Every so often Brad had his uniformed grooms lead the horse in circles, and Christina could hear the admiring coos of the crowds that drifted down the shed row.

"They've got that horse strutting around like a peacock," Dani muttered, glaring in the direction of Townsend Acres' stalls.

"None of that matters," Naomi reminded Christina cheerfully as she walked by with an armful of freshly rolled bandages. "The only thing that matters is how well Star does on race day."

"I know," Christina replied, frowning as she worked on a particularly stubborn spot on Star's bridle with her thumbnail.

Her attention was diverted from her task as she saw two reporters walk up to Star's stall. They were wearing press passes and talking loudly. One of them, a tall man with curly gray hair, gave Star a pitying glance.

"No story here, that's for sure," he said, his voice carrying above the music. "This is that has-been I read about the other day."

"Yep, that's him all right. I heard he nearly died,"

the other man said. "Actually, he looks okay. But looks can be deceiving."

The gray-haired reporter shrugged. "Why would anyone waste the fee when they know the kind of competition they're up against?"

"Owners can be crazy sometimes. They let their hearts get in the way of their good sense," the other man replied.

Christina felt hot tears burn against her eyelids. She knew she shouldn't listen to what people were saying. Still, she couldn't help wondering if maybe she had let her heart rule when it came to Star. Was he really up to this?

Walking quickly over to a pay phone at the end of the shed row, Christina dropped in several coins.

Ashleigh answered on the first ring. "Whitebrook Farm," she said.

"Mom," Christina blurted out, "it's me."

"Is everything okay?" Ashleigh asked quickly.

"Yeah," Christina replied. She drew circles in the dirt with the toe of her paddock boot.

"You don't sound okay," Ashleigh said.

Christina sighed and leaned against the wall. "I'm okay. I just have a question. Do you think I'm totally crazy to be racing Star here?"

"No," her mom said. "If I did, I never would have agreed to it. Why are you so worried? Has something happened?"

Christina wiped her eyes with the back of her hand, willing her mother's strength to seep through the phone and into her. "No," she said. "It's just that Celtic Mist set a track record when they breezed him this morning. The Townsends are bragging all over the place, and everyone's making this huge deal about it."

Ashleigh's light laugh floated into Christina's ear. "Don't pay attention to the hype. You've been around racing long enough to know what's important. All the great workouts in the world mean nothing if a horse doesn't cross the finish line first when it really counts."

When Christina didn't answer, Ashleigh said, "Right, Chris?"

"Right," Christina said quietly.

"You've never doubted Star before," her mother added. "There's no reason to start now."

Christina couldn't argue with that. Feeling her spirits lift slightly, Christina said good-bye to her mom and hung up the phone. Wandering back to Star's stall, she put her arms around his neck and scratched him gently behind the ears.

"I guess there's nothing else to do but forget about Celtic Mist and hope for the best," she told him.

Star butted her playfully with his nose. He nibbled a button on her shirt, nearly pulling it off.

"Stop it, you silly," Christina said, pushing him away. She found that she was smiling, in spite of her fears.

10

THE DAY BEFORE THE LOUISIANA DERBY, CHRISTINA WOKE early. It took her a moment to remember that she was in a motel room in New Orleans, not home in her sunny bedroom at Whitebrook. Throwing back the covers, she sat up blearily and groaned. Her head ached, and her eyes felt as scratchy as sandpaper.

She had hardly slept. The bed sagged in the middle, and all night long she had heard someone's radio blasting. The blinds were broken, and through the bent slats she could see a neon sign flashing "Catfish Joe's."

When she had finally drifted off, she dreamed she was on Star, galloping down endless tracks, falling farther and farther behind.

"Come on, Star!" she tried to yell. But her voice was stuck in her throat.

It didn't help Christina's mood any when she turned on the shower to find that it was lukewarm. Periodically blasts of scalding-hot water would course through the showerhead, causing the shivering Christina to yelp in surprise.

After she dressed, she met her parents at the motel coffee shop, where they were waiting at the counter for their coffee order. Ashleigh had flown in late the night before, and her father had just arrived.

"Good morning," her dad said brightly. "Did you sleep well?"

"Hardly," Christina declared. "I must have ridden that race in my dreams at least three times. And I never even found out how well we did. I kept waking up before the finish line."

Ashleigh sighed. "I remember those racing-anxiety dreams. Tracks that stretched to infinity. Horses that were as big as houses. People shouting to you that you were in the wrong race."

"Sounds about right," Christina said, rubbing her eyes. "But you forgot all the George clones who kept trying to force us into the rail and were beating Star with big bullwhips."

"Well, I didn't have George in my day, but I did race against some pretty nasty characters," Ashleigh said, remembering. "I used to dream the jockeys had fangs like vampires."

"The dreams were bad enough, but when I woke

up, I kept thinking about what those reporters said the other day about Star's being washed up."

"Well, he's not," Ashleigh said firmly. "And you can't let what people say get to you. There will always be gossip at the track. If you're going to survive in this business, you have to shut it out. Star's trip on the track will say it all."

"What do you want to eat?" her dad asked, motioning to the trays of baked goods by the cash register.

"Nothing," Christina mumbled. Her stomach was already rebelling against the odors wafting around the coffee shop. But her dad gave her a stern look, and she didn't feel like arguing. She grabbed a Power Bar from a basket and tried to swallow at least part of it on the way to Fair Grounds.

After they arrived at the track, Christina's parents went to the track office, and Christina headed to the Whitebrook stalls. The backside was a flurry of activity. Christina stepped aside several times to avoid grooms barreling past with laden wheelbarrows. She listened to the sounds of horses whinnying and stomping in their stalls. She could hear them munching their hay. As several Thoroughbreds went by on their way to morning workouts, Christina found herself studying them intently.

Why did each one look sleeker and fitter than the last? she wondered. She knew the answer, of course.

As the Kentucky Derby drew closer, each prep race took on more meaning. Only the stronger contenders were entered, the horses that had been winning stakes races and gearing up for glory all year long.

Star hadn't raced since that horrible day at Belmont. Closing her eyes, Christina relived that awful trip. It had been a beautiful day, and Star had been entered in a seven-furlong allowance race. He dived right out of the chute, and Christina felt sure that this would be his day. The track was fast, and Christina was pleased with how strong Star felt. He dropped to the rail, galloping along with the rest of the field. Christina knew she had to wait for just the right moment for Star to pull ahead. And she had no doubt that when the time came, the big colt would scoot away from the pack and blow them all away.

Then the trouble had started. When it was time for Star to make a move, Christina realized that the colt was giving his all just to hold his position. His strides began to feel heavy, and his breathing sounded labored. Star made a tremendous push, but it wasn't enough. He finished a disappointing seventh in a field of ten.

Right then Christina had known that something was terribly wrong. But at that moment she hadn't had any idea how sick Star really was. Only a few hours later he was struggling just to stand up.

Taking a deep breath of the sultry air, Christina

opened her eyes. She tried to remind herself that he was healthy now. It was time to shake off her worries. Star was fitter than he had ever been before. So why did she keep looking for reasons to worry? The sight of Star's coppery nose cheered her up momentarily, and she smiled when she heard his piercing whinny.

"Hey, you," she greeted him affectionately, opening his stall door and stepping inside. Hugging him, she laughed as he shoved her with his nose. "I hope you slept better than I did."

"Oh, he slept well, all right," Dani said, coming up behind her. "During the night when I peeked in on him, he was sound asleep, his lower lip hanging almost to the floor. I checked on him an hour later, and he was in the exact same position."

Christina smiled again, but as she got ready for her morning workout, her spirits once again slid down into her boots.

Dani had Star waiting for Christina at the track opening. After Christina had mounted and settled into her light exercise saddle, she looked up to see Ashleigh coming toward her.

"So the word is that the footing here is the best," Ashleigh said, double-checking the girth. "I've talked to a few other trainers, and they tell me the same thing. It's very fair."

"Good," Christina said.

After having ridden on a number of different

tracks, Christina had come to learn that each track played differently. Depending upon the weather conditions and the type of dirt used, some tracks were "cuppy," with the dirt breaking away under a horse's hooves. Other tracks would hold too much moisture and become sloppy. But as she stepped onto the freshly harrowed track, marred by only a few hoofprints, she realized that at least one thing was going her way. The footing here at Fair Grounds was firm, with the right amount of give.

The night before, when she had had trouble sleeping, Christina had flipped through a brochure about the track that someone had left on the coffee table. Along with details of Fair Grounds' colorful history, the brochure was filled with information about track specifications. There was a whole paragraph devoted to the composition of the footing. "Spillway sand" was what the locals called it. Christina shook her head. She'd read the entire brochure, hoping it would help lull her to sleep. As a result, she knew more about Fair Grounds than she knew about her home tracks.

"Now, take it easy out there today," Ashleigh warned. "This isn't the race yet."

Christina nodded and pulled her goggles down. She shifted her weight slightly forward in the saddle, asking Star for a jog. He sprang ahead, his movement light and floating. When Star was warmed up, Christina let him open up for a short distance, shooting past a couple of poles, but was careful to save him for the next day.

The nearly empty grandstands next to the track seemed large and intimidating. As Christina and Star flew down the track, Christina had a quick mental picture of how full the stands would be the next day. Her throat went dry, and her heart started banging away in her chest.

You've never been freaked out about crowds before, she reminded herself sternly.

Star began pulling at the bit, and for a moment Christina was tempted to let him go. Maybe feeling his powerful burst of speed would give her the blast of confidence she needed and allay her fears that Star wasn't up to this race. But Ashleigh was holding up her hand, so reluctantly Christina held Star in.

"Not today, big guy," she murmured. "You'll have your chance to run tomorrow."

Standing up in her stirrups, Christina brought Star back to a jog. Out of the corner of her eye she watched the other horses breezing past her.

"None of them looks as good as you do," she murmured to her colt. "Some of them might be pretty, but not one of them has your style."

Star tossed his head, his magnificent mane flowing, and Christina felt a surge of pride. She couldn't help noticing that some of the riders were watching her and looking Star over.

They're sizing up the competition, she tried to tell herself.

Christina was just taking Star off the track when she saw Celtic Mist heading toward her. His large, dark eyes were expressive, and his gray coat gleamed.

She hesitated for a split second, taking in the sight of the colt's massive muscles and alert, eager demeanor. No doubt about it—he was well bred and in fine form. No wonder the fans were going crazy and snapping his picture whenever they could. No wonder he was the press box favorite. What chance did Star have next to a horse like that?

Christina rode Star past the big colt. As she headed out through the gap, she saw Brad and Lavinia walking toward her. Lavinia was wearing a pale green suit and a huge hat with silk orchids on it.

Take that thing off before you spook every horse on the place, Christina thought. She turned Star's head slightly away so that he wouldn't catch sight of the strange-looking headgear.

When Lavinia saw Christina, she spoke loudly so that Christina could hear every word. "Oh, Brad, isn't it exciting that they're doing a prerace TV special on Celtic Mist? He's a TV star as well as a Triple Crown contender," she gushed.

"Some horses have all the luck," Brad said smoothly. He gave Christina and Star a pitying glance.

Christina looked away. Though she didn't care

about publicity, it did nothing to help her sinking feeling that she didn't really belong here. She never should have entered Star in a race like this.

Was the reporter she'd overheard earlier right? Was she one of those owners who was thinking with her heart instead of her head? Maybe she'd gotten so caught up in her dream that she'd become totally blind to reality.

Sliding off Star, Christina removed his saddle so that Dani could throw a light cooler on his back.

"I caught the last part of his workout. He looked good out there," Dani said.

"Thanks," Christina replied hollowly.

She tried to lose herself in her barn chores. First she cleaned her equipment. Afterward she checked the horses' waterers and refilled a couple of hay nets, looking for things to keep herself busy. When she was satisfied that there was nothing more to do, Christina decided to wander around the stable area. She might as well get a look at a couple of the other Derby starters. There was Reconciled, a California-bred bay colt that had won the San Vicente Stakes, and Clover Rain, a Kentucky-bred colt who'd finished second to Celtic Mist in the Fountain of Youth Stakes.

"Pretty impressive horses," she murmured to herself as she headed back to keep Star company. She wished that her stomach would calm down and that her throat didn't feel so dry. In a little over twenty-four hours she and Star would be in the starting gate. The race was fast approaching, and as every minute went by, Christina felt more irritable and jittery.

By early afternoon Christina was so nervous, she snapped at a reporter who asked her where the Townsend horse he'd heard so much about was stabled. Just after she had told the reporter to go find Celtic Mist himself, Christina saw her mom standing by the tack room. It was clear Ashleigh had heard what she'd said. Christina could see it in her mother's eyes as she walked over.

"Never let them see your nerves, Chris," Ashleigh said disapprovingly. "You know that's rule number one."

Christina scowled. "I don't care what people think."

"This is a business," her mom reminded her. "No matter how you feel, you must act professional at all times."

"I know, I know," Christina said.

Just then Naomi emerged from the tack room with a stack of rolled bandages. She stopped, glancing at Christina and then at Ashleigh. "Sorry," she muttered. "Am I interrupting something?"

"Just a lecture," Christina grumbled.

Ashleigh studied her for a moment.

"You're tired," she said firmly. Without wasting a minute, she ordered Christina back to the motel to catch up on her sleep.

"Oh, c'mon, Chris. The bags under your eyes are so big, you could stuff groceries in them," Naomi teased when Christina started to protest. "Your mom's right. Get some sleep and you'll feel better."

"I wish that's all it was," Christina muttered a while later after her dad had dropped her off at the motel.

Still, she was glad to burrow under the blanket in the darkened room. It wasn't too long before the dreams began again, though. Christina tossed and turned for an hour, until finally she threw back the covers and sat up.

Drawing back the curtains to let the sun in, Christina sat gloomily on the scratchy sofa, wondering what to do next. She shoved aside the track brochure sitting on the coffee table. She didn't want to read any more about track footing, that was for sure. She considered flipping through the racing magazines the motel had provided, but she decided against it. The last thing she needed to do was be reminded that very soon she'd be out there, getting ready to ride Star to a disappointing loss.

She wondered if she should catch her parents as soon as they returned to the motel and tell them she'd made a terrible mistake coming here.

I'll just tell them I'm sorry, Christina thought. *I never should have pressured Mom into letting me enter Star in a race as big as the Louisiana Derby. We'll just go home. I should be grateful that Star is well and can run at all.*

The next minute Christina let out her breath in an explosive whoosh. Star's incredible workout times weren't figments of her imagination. They *had* happened. They meant something. They meant that Star was ready for more than a few local, unchallenging races.

Hugging a pillow to her chest, Christina stared at the wall. It was so confusing. If Star was destined to race in a competitive race such as the Louisiana Derby, why did she feel so scared?

Why was the pressure of this race getting to her so much? she wondered. After all, she'd ridden in lots of important races before. She'd won a few, but she'd lost lots of races, too.

If only I had someone to talk to, Christina thought. Suddenly she decided to call Parker.

No, that wouldn't help a bit, she realized. Things seemed different between them. Maybe it was because she knew Parker didn't approve of her plans for the future. Maybe they would talk it out after the race and everything would be okay again. But for now, she didn't think he could make her feel better. He might even make her feel worse.

She couldn't talk to Melanie, either. Melanie was probably on a horse at Gulfstream, or maybe kicking back with Jazz. None of her friends at school would understand, either, although they'd certainly try.

There was no one, no one except . . .

Lyssa! Christina sat up straight at the thought. *Of course!* Lyssa Hynde knew Star. She knew what they had been through. She certainly understood stiff competition.

Rummaging through her duffel bag, Christina located her address book and punched in Lyssa's number.

Please be there, she thought as she waited for someone to pick up. The odds that Lyssa would be hanging around the ranch when she had so much work to do were not good.

"Hello?" It was Lyssa's voice.

"Hi, it's Christina. I can't believe I got hold of you," Christina said in a rush. Suddenly she heard a loud moo, and she pulled the phone away from her ear.

Lyssa's laughter rang out. "I'm here in the barn with Sylvester. He's the cutest little Hereford. He was born just a week ago, and I'm bottle-feeding him. His mama decided she didn't want him."

Christina brought the phone back to her ear. "That's sad."

"That's life," Lyssa said philosophically. "Where there are animals, there's trouble."

"Isn't that the truth," Christina agreed ruefully.

"Is something wrong? Where are you, anyway?"

"I'm in New Orleans," Christina replied. "There's nothing wrong. It's just that I'm running in the Louisiana

Derby tomorrow, and Lyssa, I'm scared to death."

"You're kidding, right? The famous Christina Reese, scared to race?"

"Stop joking. I'm serious."

"Tell me about it," came Lyssa's voice, immediately sympathetic.

"There's not much to tell," admitted Christina. "I was so sure Star was ready for this race that I really pushed my mom to let me enter him. Now that we're here, I can't help wondering if I've made the biggest mistake of my life. I'm just not sure if he's up to it."

Lyssa said, "Are you forgetting what I told you? Have you been establishing yourself as the *itancan* so that he'll follow your leadership?"

Christina scowled. "I haven't forgotten. But I keep having these dreams, and sometimes I ride through the race in my mind, and I picture Star flagging and—and falling farther behind. It's awful."

Lyssa was silent for a moment. "Let me get this straight. Star's totally better, he's been working well for the past few weeks, and he's turned in some of his fastest times ever. What does your mom think?"

"She thinks he's good to go. So does everybody else at Whitebrook."

Lyssa's voice was impatient. "And you're wondering if he's up to this race?"

Christina cradled the phone with her shoulder and toyed with the blind cord. "That about sums it up. I keep picturing the headlines that say, 'Celtic Mist Glides to Big Easy Win.'"

"Do you realize how lame that sounds?"

"Yup," Christina replied. "Which is why I called you."

"Good thing. You need a reality sandwich, and you're gonna get it."

Christina smiled at the mental picture her friend was creating. "Bring it on," she cracked.

"This isn't funny," Lyssa said. "You've spent years getting this horse ready. The two of you have been through thick and thin. He's primed and ready to rock, but you're set on making him lose."

"*What?*" Christina couldn't believe what she was hearing. "I am not!"

"Well, it's pretty simple, if you ask me. If you're sitting around fretting and picturing Star dogging it, and you're listening to all the blabber flying around the racetrack, you're not taking care of business. The way I see it, you're not preparing to win—you're mentally rehearsing losing. Keep doing that, and I guarantee you won't like the results."

Christina scowled and bit her lip. The way Lyssa put it, that was exactly what she was doing. Planning a loss—and at a time when she needed a win more than ever!

Then came the kicker. "Do you think that's fair to Star?"

144

Christina sat bolt upright on the bed. "Of course not!"

"See?" said Lyssa happily. "You sorted it out yourself. You didn't need me."

Christina chuckled, shaking her head. "No, you're wrong," she said softly. "I did need you to give it to me straight."

"Well, whatever." Suddenly Lyssa's voice sounded strained. "Oh, rats, I've gotta go. One of our guests' horses just galloped riderless into the corral here."

"Oh, gosh," Christina exclaimed. "I hope everything's okay. Thanks for all your help. And don't worry, I'll straighten myself out."

"I know you will." With that, the phone clicked and Lyssa was gone.

But her words stayed with Christina for hours. She closed her eyes and pictured herself on the track with Star. Forcing herself to relax, she imagined Star breaking cleanly from the starting gate and running his fastest. She pictured Star overtaking Celtic Mist and whipping past the finish line in first place. She ran through the race several times in her mind, each time envisioning a sweeping victory. She fell asleep with a big smile on her face and slept till morning.

When Christina woke up on race day, she knew deep down that she was ready.

11

THE MORNING OF THE LOUISIANA DERBY DAWNED CLEAR and sunny. Christina had arrived at the track early and was standing in Star's stall when first light broke. The air was beginning to feel heavy and warm, and Christina felt the sweat drip from her temples.

The track was charged with excitement. TV trucks were parked next to the backside, and people were scurrying this way and that. It was clear the Louisiana Derby was a huge deal at Fair Grounds.

"Today's the big day, boy," Christina whispered, peering out of Star's stall at the commotion.

Star snorted as if to say, *No problem.*

"You're not worried, are you, boy? You're going to be awesome," Christina said, patting his neck affectionately.

146

A short while later she went out to the track and leaned against the rail. Watching the harrows making their way up and down the deep, rich dirt, Christina listened to the workers laughing and talking among themselves. She glanced at a few nearby "rail birds," spectators who had arrived early to watch the morning workouts. How lucky she was to be part of the track family—it was so much better to be part of the action than just to watch!

Of course, it might be less nerve-wracking to be a spectator right now, Christina thought, wiping back some sweaty wisps of hair. *Sure, I might have to worry about losing some money on a horse. But I wouldn't have to worry about letting my horse down.*

Shaking her head, she reminded herself to think like a winner, just as Lyssa had told her to.

A TV camera operator set up her equipment next to where Christina was standing and began to film the prerace action on the track. A well-dressed announcer spoke into a microphone, describing the work being done on the track. Christina moved down the rail so she wouldn't be in the way, but she could still hear what the announcer was saying.

"As you can see, a lot of care goes into prepping Fair Grounds for race day," the announcer said in a deep voice, gesturing toward the activity taking place on the track. "You might not know it, but there are a number of people with unusual jobs who work behind the scenes to make sure each race is run fairly. And now we turn our camera toward one such important member of the track staff."

Christina watched as the camera operator trained her lens on a short, balding man. "This is Clyde Marsden," the announcer said smoothly. "He's Fair Grounds' track identifier, the staffer in charge of making sure the right horse arrives in the paddock. Clyde, will you describe your all-important function to our viewers?"

Christina listened as the track identifier explained how he checked each horse's lip tattoo to make sure the horse entered in the race was indeed the same as the horse led into the saddling paddock.

The announcer cut in. "A Thoroughbred is tattooed with a letter, signifying its birth year, and five digits that correspond to its registration number."

"Believe me, there are a lot of horses that object to me pulling on their lips," Clyde said when the mike was thrust back toward him. "I've been kicked and knocked to the ground more times than I care to count. I don't even want to *think* about the number of times I've been pawed and head-whipped."

Out of the corner of her eye, Christina saw the camera turn to another staff member, a tall, thin man with a grave face.

"This is the track chaplain, Ned Meyers," the announcer said. "I don't suppose your job is to pray for a winner, is it?"

148

"No," Ned answered with a sad chuckle. "My line of work is giving guidance to backside workers who face emotional or spiritual crises. The backside of a racetrack is like a small city. Everyone has a place, but sometimes they lose their way. That's where I come in. But believe me, it's not always easy."

As Christina listened, she felt a growing respect for the track staffers. She had been around tracks all her life, so it was easy to take things for granted. She'd never realized how many people it took to keep the races running smoothly. She had been so busy worrying about whether Star was fit to run in the Derby, but now she realized that there were lots of other people who had their share of race-day hassles, too. And in the end, *they* didn't have the satisfaction of owning a wonderful horse such as Star—no matter what the tote board said.

And I do, she thought happily.

Listening to the track staffers' concerns had helped Christina put her fears into perspective, and when she headed toward the track kitchen to meet her parents, she felt calmer than ever.

Ashleigh and Mike were seated at the end of a long table, studying the program. Christina grabbed a carton of yogurt and an energy bar from the lunch counter and joined her parents.

"Nervous?" her dad asked when she sat down next to him.

"Nuh-uh," Christina replied confidently, opening her yogurt container.

"You're lying," Mike said teasingly.

Christina shook her head. "I *was* nervous, but I'm over it now," she said. "Star and I are going to do our best, and that's all I can ask."

"Good girl," Ashleigh said approvingly. She glanced at the race program spread out in front of her.

Christina noticed her mother was wearing a brightly colored orchid in the lapel of her jacket. Closing her eyes, Christina tried to visualize Star surrounded by orchids in the winner's circle.

Prepare to win. That's what Lyssa had said to do.

Ashleigh shoved the program under her nose, pulling her out of her fantasy. "Hmmm. The race analyst is playing it safe. 'Though Wonder's Star, by Jazzman and out of Derby winner Ashleigh's Wonder, has been out of action for several months, this horse has shown promise and could surprise.'"

Christina laughed. "*Surprise.* That word again. I'll bet the fortune-teller Katie hired gave him that hot tip," she said. "Well, at least the analyst didn't call him a has-been like everyone else around here."

Mike took the program and studied it while he ate. "We drew the number-five post position. Not great, but passable."

"You'll have to play it smart," Ashleigh added. "But you already know what to do."

"I'll be fine, Mom," Christina said with a grin.

Ashleigh sipped her coffee and stood up. "Well, the circus ought to be starting soon. I'll go keep the horses company."

By the time Christina left the kitchen and headed for the Whitebrook stalls, she saw what her mom meant when she used the word *circus*. The admission gates weren't open, but even more television crews were setting up cameras on the backside. Reporters were milling around, stopping trainers and jockeys and asking questions. Christina felt a couple of journalists' eyes turn in her direction, but no one made a move to bring their mikes over to her. George Valdez, she noticed, was surrounded by reporters.

Fine by me, Christina thought. *He can brag all he wants. Star and I will just keep quiet and win.*

Anyway, she told herself, the last thing she needed was some pushy reporter saying something that would get her upset all over again. She had had enough of that over the last few weeks. It was time to concentrate on the race.

Christina spent the rest of the morning grooming Star until he gleamed like burnished copper. As she picked out each of his feet, she mentally rode the race, picturing Star breaking away from the pack on the stretch.

"Fair Grounds has the second-longest stretch in the country," she told Star. "You'll like that, boy—

plenty of ground to blast past the field."

Star appeared unconcerned as he nibbled on her shirt playfully. Christina finished up by rubbing a soft cloth over his coat. There was nothing more to do until just before the race, and standing around would only frazzle her nerves, Christina knew, so she decided to take a walk.

Walking around the grounds, she stopped among the crowds to admire the white obelisks marking the graves of two track greats: Black Gold, who had won the Kentucky Derby years ago, and Pan Zareta, another Fair Grounds favorite. After a while she drifted over to the grandstand area and caught a glimpse of the crowds streaming toward their seats.

All too soon it was time to head to the jockeys' locker room. As she made her way through the throng of spectators to change into her silks, she wished Melanie or her jockey friend Vicky Frontiere were there to talk to. But most of the jockeys she knew were in Florida. The ones at Fair Grounds all seemed to know each other, and they ignored her as she made her way to the women's changing room—all except George, who smirked at her when he walked past on his way to the steam room.

Don't let him get to you, Christina chided herself. But it was no use. She could feel her stomach churning.

Stripping off her street clothes, Christina changed into her blue-and-white silks, her throat dry and her heart pounding as she dressed. She hardly noticed the other jockeys' bantering as they changed or the whoops that went up from the main room outside as still others watched the races on the TV there. It was all so surreal. As she walked out of the changing area carrying the worn racing saddle that had once been her mother's, she walked past the door of the steam room, from which George had just come out, rubbing his shoulder.

"Hey," he called out to her. "You be sure you stay in the right lane so you and yesterday's news don't get hurt."

Christina's cheeks flamed at the insult. She knew that George was insinuating that Star was slow and that he ought to stay wide so he wouldn't get in the way of the faster horses on the rail.

A couple of the other jockeys and track staff looked over, waiting for her reaction. And though Christina knew her mom would have advised her to simply walk away, her mind flashed to Lyssa's face. Lyssa wouldn't let anyone get away with a crack like that.

"Choke on our dust," she retorted, smiling sweetly.

George's eyebrows shot up, and he sniggered as he walked away.

Christina had weighed in and joined the other jockeys as they made their way to the viewing paddock. She handed her saddle to Ashleigh, who took it to the saddling area, then walked over to Dani to watch Mike lead Star around the viewing paddock. The noise of the crowd gathering around the paddock was deafening.

"Oh, look, there's Wonder's Star. He's the one who's going to win." The voice of a little girl carried high above the noise of the fans. Christina tried to pick out her face in the crowd, but she couldn't see who she was.

Funny, Christina thought, turning to face Star as he came around the paddock, *that little girl sounded so sure. Well, why not?* Christina's throat tightened as she glimpsed her magnificent colt prancing in the sun beside her father. He looked every inch a champion.

After Star made his second round around the viewing paddock, Mike stopped him in front of Christina. Dani hoisted her into the tiny racing saddle, and Christina placed her feet in the stirrups. As she settled into the rhythm of Star's familiar stride, she heard the little voice again.

"That's the horse, Daddy. Let's stand by the finish line so we can watch him win."

This time Christina didn't try to find her. She didn't need to see the little girl's face to know just how much she believed in Star. And if a perfect stranger could believe in Star, then surely she could. After all, she had raised him from a baby!

The pony rider, a large, suntanned man who looked like he'd never smiled in his life, fell in next to her, riding a stocky pinto. He clipped a lead onto Star's bridle and led them onto the track.

Christina breathed deeply. "Well, here we go, boy," she said, her teeth chattering in spite of her attempts to remain calm. If only her stomach weren't doing flip-flops. She wondered fleetingly if she might get sick, but then shook her head and mentally commanded her stomach to behave.

Star pranced a little as jazz music burst through the loudspeakers, and the pony rider stayed close, watching for any sign that Star might try to break away. Christina leaned forward and stroked the chestnut's neck, which had broken out in an excited sweat.

"He's feeling good, isn't he?" the man grunted.

"Yeah," Christina replied. "I hope your friends put some money on him today."

The man gave her a sour look. "I never forget the words of the great trainer Charlie Whittingham: 'A good horse is like a strawberry. It can spoil overnight.'"

Christina laughed at the old track witticism. "Well, this big guy is ripe and ready to run."

Soon they were galloping along the track for their warm-up. Star was responding beautifully, and Christina could feel his body tensing with excitement.

He danced all the way over to the reddish orange

starting gate. When it was Star's turn to load into the number five chute, Christina felt her stomach start to churn again.

Oh, why did I ever decide to be a jockey? she wondered for a split second as Star scooted in and the gate slammed behind them.

Because I'd never want to do anything else, she reminded herself quickly. A dry mouth, a queasy stomach, and nerves that wouldn't quit were just part of it.

Christina tried to shut out the rustling noises of the horses next to her and the sounds of the jockeys' voices as they tried to soothe their anxious mounts. Hastily she shoved her goggles down and looked at the expanse of track visible to her through the openings in the gate. It would be a fast track, that much she knew.

After that, there was no time to think of anything else but breaking clean the moment the gates opened. Christina concentrated on focusing her entire body and mind for the next few all-important seconds.

Claaaaang! The bell that had rung in her sleep weeks ago sounded. Mercifully, it was considerably shorter, and the gate flew open in seconds.

Star broke cleanly, and Christina felt herself swept along in the throng of hurtling horses thundering down the track.

Watch for an opening. A gray horse and a bay parted in front of her, and her brain screamed, *Now!*

Within seconds she had pushed her way over to the rail, conscious that Celtic Mist and Reconciled were the only two horses ahead of Star.

Rate him. Feel it, don't think. Christina heard her mother's instructions as clearly as if Ashleigh were riding right along with her. She tried to sit perfectly still so that she wouldn't send any confusing signals with her body that might distract Star.

Frowning, she realized that Star was moving up too early. Star was a come-from-behind horse. He ran best at the middle of the pack, saving his speed for the homestretch.

But this day he seemed to have something different in mind. Though Christina struggled valiantly to pace him, Star continued gaining ground, staying well ahead of Clover Rain and Gottagetthere as they swept past the first turn.

It was too soon to make a move, Christina knew. They still had a long way to go. And then there was that long stretch that the Fair Grounds track was so famous for.

Momentarily the announcer's voice penetrated her brain. "And it's Celtic Mist in the lead, with Reconciled challenging, and Wonder's Star, who appears to be ready to put on some pressure, in the number three spot."

Christina kept Star rated in the second turn, feeling the dirt from the horses' hooves pelting her goggles, still dismayed to find Star so far up in the field.

"Take it easy, big guy," Christina called out.

How much does he have left? she wondered as they thundered down the backstretch and into the far turn. She knew the moment of truth would come when she asked for that next burst of speed. There would be no turning back. If Star couldn't sustain the pace, if he fell back even momentarily, he'd never pass the front-runners.

Visualize a win! Remember the itancan. *Star will follow your lead.*

With that, Christina let out a little more rein, and Star shifted gears. She felt his legs pumping under her, and when they hit the final stretch, she knew it was time.

Reconciled was tiring and falling farther behind Celtic Mist. Christina waited until Reconciled drifted wide.

Now! Christina crouched low over Star's neck and let him go. He moved up along the rail, squeezing past Reconciled and gaining on Celtic Mist.

This is it! Star was trying his hardest, running his heart out, giving everything he had left. They were hurtling along at an impressive speed, but there was still a way to go up the stretch, which seemed endless. She could only hope that Celtic Mist would tire as well and drop down enough so that Star could pass him at the finish line.

The next second Christina felt herself thrown up onto Star's shoulder as he put on another burst of speed.

Where did that come from? Christina thought with a shock as Star's powerful legs carried them up next to Celtic Mist's shoulder.

"That's it!" she cried to Star. "Come on, boy, you can do it!"

"And it's Wonder's Star looming dangerously as Celtic Mist struggles to keep his lead. Number three, Reconciled, drops back, with Clover Rain easing up," the announcer called.

"Give it up, loser," Christina heard Celtic Mist's jockey yell at her.

The roar from the stands was deafening as George brought his whip down on Celtic Mist, but Star continued to keep up with him. Christina gripped her reins and kneaded her hands into his mane. She could feel Clover Rain come up behind them in the same instant she felt Star drop back.

"No!" she called out.

This was what she had been afraid of. Star had given it his all, but had it been too soon?

Suddenly Celtic Mist dropped back, too. Christina was surprised, but she pressed on, sensing that Clover Rain was continuing to gain ground.

"We can't lose this now. Come on, Star, I know you can do it! I *know* you can!" Christina cried, asking Star to find a tiny bit more.

The *itancan* had shown the way, and now it was up to Star to follow the instincts of his ancestors.

This was the moment when years of love, tears, and training came together.

As Star ran, Christina felt herself transported miles away from the Fair Grounds track. In her mind's eye she was riding her beloved chestnut over the familiar grassy fields of Whitebrook. The sun was warming her shoulders as the big colt galloped effortlessly, the two of them an inseparable team. Leafy trees flew past as she and Star ran toward their destiny.

Suddenly the roar of the stands broke into Christina's consciousness, and instantly visions of Whitebrook disappeared. The finish line loomed ahead.

"Attaboy, Star!" Christina shouted at the top of her lungs.

Star responded as he kicked in for home, his ground-eating strides pulling away slowly but surely from his only challenger, Clover Rain, by half a length, then a length. He was now closing in on the finish line, continuing to pull ahead of the field.

In the next instant, Christina felt only the exhilaration of crossing the line.

"And Wonder's Star has it. Wonder's Star wins the Louisiana Derby by a length!" the announcer cried out.

Christina rode on and began pulling up, her heart pounding in her ears. When she was finally able to persuade Star to come back to a jog, she leaned down and hugged him as hard as she could.

Closing her eyes, Christina absorbed the cheers from the stands. She knew she was grinning like an idiot, but it didn't matter. The only thing that mattered was that Star had done his best and shown everyone what a winner he really was.

Star shook his head, trying to evade the bit as Christina kept him from breaking back into a canter. When she was finally able to get him to circle, she rode him back toward the grandstand.

The outrider tipped his velvet cap as he rode up to meet her. "You sure surprised a few folks here today," he said.

"I was kind of surprised myself. Not by the win, though," Christina said as the outrider helped keep Star down to a jog. It was *how* Star had won that Christina was surprised by. Star had never raced like that before, staying close to the front and making such a bold move at the end.

Ha! she thought. *So maybe that fortune-teller wasn't so fake after all. She knew there was a surprise in my future. This was it!*

Christina laughed aloud, savoring the sweetness of the moment. This day would remain forever in her mind as the day Star had made believers out of everyone!

"Well, Chris, I guess we'll have to get you two

ready for Churchill Downs in May," Ashleigh said, a broad grin on her face, as Christina rode up in a blur of happiness.

Christina beamed down at her mom, who had grabbed Star's bridle and was leading them into the winner's circle.

Kentucky Derby, here we come!

12

THE CROWD CONTINUED TO ROAR FROM THE GRANDSTANDS. A jazz band struck up, but it was almost drowned out by the deafening crowd. With tears welling up in her eyes and fogging up her goggles, Christina whispered to Star, "That's for you, big guy."

Star tossed his head proudly, sending out a shower of foam. He arched his neck and pranced. Christina laughed at his antics, still having trouble believing what had just happened. Her colt had beaten the odds. He had risen above the dismal expectations of almost everyone to win the Louisiana Derby!

If only that know-it-all from the Racing Reporter *could see us now*, Christina thought.

A couple of jockeys called out their congratulations, and Christina raised her hand in appreciation.

Clover Rain's jockey saluted her briefly with his hand up by his helmet.

Now that's something, Christina thought, returning his salute. Jockeys could be a competitive group. Very few of them would be so sporting about coming in second in such a disappointing loss.

"I wouldn't get too excited. It ain't over yet," snarled George Valdez from behind her. He pointed his whip at Christina. Christina noticed that the Townsend silks were covered in mud.

Christina's eyes widened.

"It *is* over, George," Ashleigh insisted. "Give it up."

"You'd never have beaten us if Celtic Mist hadn't stumbled," George growled, and jogged away.

Instantly Christina's heart lodged in her throat. Was George going to lodge a made-up complaint with the track officials? How could he? She and Star had already pulled ahead when he and Celtic Mist fell back. They had never jostled each other. Had something happened without her knowing?

Glancing at the tote board, she was relieved to see that the lights weren't flashing. There didn't appear to be an inquiry. And now the announcer was saying that the results were official. Star had won.

When they reached the winner's circle, Christina patted Star's sweat-soaked neck again as her dad and Dani rushed out to meet them. Christina dismounted, then removed her helmet for a moment to push back her sweaty hair.

Mike swept Christina up in a hug. "You did it!" he cried.

"You mean *Star* did it!" Christina corrected him.

Dani hugged her quickly, then made a huge fuss over the big chestnut colt. "Extra carrots for you tonight," she said, reaching up to stroke his lathered neck.

"Mom, what happened with Celtic Mist?" Christina whispered urgently to Ashleigh.

"Not to worry," her mom said while Christina pulled off her racing saddle. "This was your day. Mist stumbled way after he had fallen behind you. Brad made a fuss and started blaming people right and left, but the stewards didn't find anything to contest. George is just sour, that's all."

Mike added, "Forget about George and enjoy your win."

Christina giggled. "Well, I have to confess I kind of enjoyed seeing the Townsend silks covered in mud," she whispered to her father.

Too bad it wasn't Brad wearing them, she thought. Well, she'd have to describe it in great, grimy detail when she called Melanie later to tell her what had happened.

Christina walked over to stand on the scales and

took the saddle when it was handed to her, still shocked by Star's amazing victory. When she stepped off, she handed the saddle to her mom, who put it back on Star. Then Ashleigh boosted her up on Star, and the cameras began to snap away.

Christina sat straight and tall on her colt, clutching the big cup they had won. Star preened for the cameras and even gave a throaty whicker when the cascade of orchids was draped over his shoulder.

"Oh, Star. How could I ever have doubted you?" Christina whispered, twining his mane in her fingers.

She and her mother exchanged proud, happy glances.

"There's only one thing that will top these orchids," Christina murmured to Ashleigh.

Ashleigh smiled knowingly even before Christina added, "Red roses!"

KARLE DICKERSON grew up riding, reading, writing, and dreaming about horses. This is the fourth horse book she has written. She's shown in hunters and dressage, worked at a Thoroughbred breeding farm, and has been on cattle drives in Wyoming. She and her family used to own a horse ranch, and have always had numerous horses and ponies. The latest include two Thoroughbreds off the track named Cezanne and Earl Gray and a gray Welsh pony named Magpie.